The Last Memory

Annette Stephenson

Acknowledgments

Thank you to family and friends for loving support as I compose beautiful stories. To each of my readers for enjoying every journey. It is a pleasure to bring characters to life that we relate to. To my loving husband; for love and inspiration for 41 years.

Love to my children Oliver, Jacob, Kamara. I love you with all my strength and devotion. You have made me proud. To my seven grandchildren.

Since I was young, I loved adventures that inspire and give hope through adversity. This book is dedicated to those who need to share a happy ending. Copyright 2022

*P*rologue

What drives a young woman to become an investigative journalist? Tess Charlton had always been interested in stories with mystery and intrigue. Her childhood dream was to be a media reporter and she worked hard throughout her school years to gain the experience needed for a career. Before getting her bachelor's degree in communication and journalism, Tess entered competitions with investigative journalist organizations such as the Online Journalism Awards. It looked good on her resume along with writing samples in her portfolio. Her high school developed a career center where she applied for internship. In college, she was provided additional resources designed for professional development. She attended workshops and courses that supplemented her undergraduate program and learned first-hand from the industry. Later, she created podcasts, television interviews, and eventually landed a job as a media reporter. Her writing skills, professional newsgathering, and proficiency showcased her talent. Her life centered around one goal, to be the best journalist out there and she was recognized for her accomplishments as she reached the top. Tess took risks as far as she could while looking into the face of danger. No story was out of reach and she pushed to investigate the many mysteries yet undiscovered. She was usually careful and quick as a cat.

Her last investigation revealed something so big that it nearly killed her. Her life changed instantly. Tess took on a new persona, a figure even she couldn't recognize. Hidden events led her into a new life full of questions. Completely on her own, unable to use her reporting skills, she needed to find a way to survive and maybe get her life back. She turned desperate, searching for clues. Life started again as a blur when she woke up from the accident. Sitting in that car was Tess and her last memory.

Chapter 1

A Woman Who Loved Intrigue

Tess Charlton came home late in the evening from a piece she finished researching about organic foods and organizations trying to stop pesticide use. After she put the coffee on, she went back to her bedroom past the clutter on her nightstand. A glass bottle of Coke sat next to a stack of mystery novels, a box of Kleenex and her glasses. The hamper was full of dirty laundry. Her boots were crusted with mud and pieces of grass clinging to the suede. She would make her bed later. Sitting on the kitchen counter, was a pile of unopened mail. She had been away from home for a few days and from the looks of it, she needed to take some days off to catch up, maybe even take some time for herself. Just hearing the espresso machine grind and steam, awakened her senses.

There were too many voicemails to answer. First on her list, was her mother, Sarah. Tess had a very close relationship with her and kept in touch even when Tess was out of town. It was obvious that a lot of energy went into her career, but that never stopped her from calling every few days, confirming that she was safe.

From the time she was little, Tess had her head in a book with twists and mystery. She collected a series of Nancy Drew and The Hardy Boys that fueled her desire to be the best at what she wanted to do with her life. On her bookshelf, was a detective kit her father gave her when he noticed how much she loved exploring clues. She won competitions in school for her research on forensics and ability to solve various situations, eventually becoming the editor of the school newspaper. After high school, it was her dream to work for a paper called The News Day as an intern. She had thoughts of having her very own column. After years of working hard, she finally reached that goal. Before she settled on where her feet were meant to be planted, Tess went abroad searching for stories worth telling. She reported in Afghanistan during the frightening wars that severely affected the lives of adults and children. She became friends with victims who tearfully told their story about the loss and fear they experienced. She toured countries where devastating earthquakes shook and once in Thailand to cover the deadly tsunami where families tried to recover after the search. She cried with mothers who lost their children. It was all they had to give them hope for their future. She slept on bare concrete floors and went into hiding when it was too dangerous to go out. Photographs of the faces of innocent children gave her the drive to continue reporting what the public needed to know. Tess wanted to make a difference in the lives of those who lived in the havoc.

Her parents lived in their own fear, hoping that their daughter would come home safe and sound each time. It was painful living with the uncertainty of her return. With careful thought, Tess decided to give up her fast life overseas. She became part of a team excelling in gathering local information that readers would find newsworthy. Tess was a risk taker, a woman who believed in doing all she could to see justice served. She always hoped that her career would make a better world and bring fairness to the voice not being heard. Locals and others loved her column and it helped the newspaper thrive, increasing readership. Because of her gift exposing real issues, some also disliked her. Tess was real and not afraid to reveal what she discovered.

She was seen out investigating with a khaki bag over her shoulder that looked like a small backpack. Inside was her purse, camera, recorder, an unused can of mace, pens and two or three small notepads. Preparation gave her confidence. She felt no need to fabricate or stretch facts for prestige. She knew that hard-found research made for great reporting.

Her assistant, Margo, had left several messages. Even though the next day was Tess's day off, she still had a meeting scheduled with her Editor in Chief, Digby Stone, a tough, but kind editor who knew how to run a paper. He was more than impressed by Tess's resume. Digby had been in the business most of his life. His father was also an editor and had an eye for hiring the best reporters. At age sixty, Digby never gave a thought to retiring. Like Tess, it was his passion.

Morning rolled around too quickly and still in her pajamas; Tess poured her coffee. Black, always black. Her dad often said it sharpened her wits. Outside, she picked up the newspaper and looked for her article. She cut out her latest column and secured it in a full scrapbook. Her home office was not an office at all. A table next to the kitchen suited her best. Stacks of papers and books collected until she finished a project that required reorganizing. On the wall next to it, hung her framed accomplishments and awards for investigations.

She heard a knock at the door and recognized the pattern.

"Margo, what are you doing here? Why didn't you call first?"

"I did call, many times. Why didn't you answer my messages?" Margo followed Tess into the apartment.

Margo had an eye for fashion and always dressed well. She looked Tess up and down as she came inside.

"I must have had it on silent. You know how I get when I'm in the zone. I was focused on this assignment for the last three days," Tess explained as she looked through her mail.

"I know. Since I didn't hear back from you, I sent Digby the last article you wrote. I had to."

"The one I haven't approved yet? It wasn't ready."

"I know, but I think it's worth it to have him read it."

"You know, Margo, no one found out who lit those fires in Julian yet. It's sad. I'm pretty sure it's a ring of arsonists. One of the houses had a husband and wife who died inside."

"I think that's what your meeting is about. Digs might want you to milk it. You're that good!"

"I've been thinking about it and I'm still not sure where I would get more information on the motive."

"Really, the woman who is able to crack just about every case. You should have been a detective," Margo complimented as she grabbed a coffee cup for herself.

"Yeah, I've been curious about this since I saw it on the news."

"Maybe you should go there, talk to some of the people."

"I thought about that. I better talk to Digby first. He's particular when it comes to the hard hitting stories. I got a feeling he won't let me write it the way I want."

"It's a risk. You like risks. You have to convince him to let you write it."

"I better get ready to meet him. I'm not sure what he's going to say about it."

"I sent out your emails yesterday. Do you need me to come with you?"

"No. Digby sounded like it was not very important."

"What are you going to do if he refuses to let you research it?"

"If I answer that, it may get me into trouble."

Margo finished her coffee and grinned, "Good answer. I gotta go. Please feel free to listen to my messages in the future."

"I'll work on it."

"It will make my job easier. Call you later," Margo said.

Tess looked at her room. The bed was still a mess and dishes were piled in the sink. It would have to wait. She pulled her hair into a ponytail and prepared to hear what was coming. Her style was either sneakers or heavy duty boots, useful when traveling to countries with uneven terrain. Jeans and a T-shirt were the easy ensemble, good for every kind of story. She was comfortable and kind. When it came to her job, she was straight forward with what she wanted. It was easy to recognize her passion when she worked aggressively and thorough. Tess couldn't stop thinking about the mystery she was sure she could crack. Reports speculated that a rash of fires were deliberately started and was assumed to be an arson's dirty work. No one in town saw what happened or would guess why. It spiked Tess's curiosity and she pitched the idea to her assistant, Margo. Because Tess was good at her job, she was expecting Digby to understand. Of all people, he should want her to investigate that assignment.

She took the elevator up to her office floor and was quickly welcomed with a good morning by everyone she worked with. Through the glass doors at the other end, she could see Digby. Wearing a white shirt with rolled up sleeves and black suspenders, he was bent looking at some papers, possibly the emails from Margo. His glasses were at the tip of his nose as she knocked at the door. He waved her in.

"Good morning, Digby."

"Is it? I liked the article on the pesticide ban. Very thorough and expected. I mean that in a good way. We should be able to get a whole week's worth of columns out of it."

"Thanks. I'm ready to work on something bigger."

"I know. I got the email from Margo."

His room was cluttered and dirty windows overlooked the city. On his desk was a small stand with his name. Digby got it from a mentor he worked with as a young man. He was told, "Every newsman should have a catchy nickname." He wanted to believe it was because of his ability to dig up information for his best stories. He liked it better than his real name, Walton Stone.

"Digby, what do you think? I need to interview some of the folks from that town and find out who started those fires."

"Tess, you're an excellent reporter. You get it done better than anyone I've worked with. But this is dangerous, I mean really dangerous! I want you to back out and let the authorities handle it. It's their job to solve these things, then you can report on it."

"Digs, you know I can do it. I've handled much worse. Remember that mob that was dumping harmful waste in the ocean? I got it done and they arrested the guys who did it."

"Yes, and that was risky." He sighed, "I want you around. It's one thing to be a good writer and reporter, but it's another thing to risk getting killed. I'm sorry, I'm going to have to say no to this one."

"You know this has been going on for a while. A couple died in that fire and to just let it go will eat me alive. I will be extra careful with this one. I don't want it to happen to anyone else's family."

"Tess, I understand you care. It is a sad loss, but we are in the news business. We can do reporting, but we can't save everyone. I know it's your passion. If these are professional arsonists, it means they are also dangerous criminals. You know what happened to the last reporter who tried to cover that story."

"Yes, I know. He was a good kid. They never found proof he was killed by them."

"Maybe not, but you know there's a big chance he was."

"I want to do this, Digby. Please let me take this one. Robbie was my friend."

"Your persistence is appreciated, but the answer is still no. I won't take that risk and you shouldn't either. It's not our job to get so involved. There's a reason for that."

"Is there anything else?" she quizzed sarcastically.

"Yes, your next assignment, will be emailed to you tomorrow. Have a nice day off."

"Have you always been this mean?" Tess asked with a slight smile.

"Yes. Now leave. I need to get some real work done."

"Digs, call for you on line two," Manny announced.

"Tomorrow," Digby reminded as he pointed at her.

She didn't want to listen. In her heart, she knew she could find out who was responsible for causing the misery. Why were arsonists targeting Julian? So far, the authorities were not solving the crime. Tess formulated a plan to do what she must to help restore a small town back to its former glory. She knew if she snooped around, there was a chance she could lose her job and her life. Digby was close to her and her family. She didn't want to betray his trust in her, but she had to have this one. It appeared that nothing was getting done and the police stopped investigating. If she really put her instincts to good use, she could be the one to solve it. At the same time, she could solve the murder of a young man named Robbie Carnes, a good friend of the news team. She wanted justice to come to him and his family and it was going to be up to her to give back what no one seemed to care about.

Chapter 2

The Risk

Tess arrived at the outlet store to meet her mom. They liked to shop together. After Tess's absence, Sarah's worries were reduced by getting together. She assured her mother she would not be traveling anytime soon. When she explained the article about the arsons, it raised Sarah's anxiety again.

"Tess, sometimes I think your job is just too dangerous."

"It could be, but I am a smart woman."

"I don't doubt that, dear. I still worry about you. Things can happen."

"Do you remember the reports about the Julian fires?"

"Yes. It was so sad to hear about them. Those poor families. It's strange how no one was ever caught."

"Not yet. I asked Digby to let me cover the story, you know, investigate and get some clues."

"Tess, are you insane? You're not qualified to handle a case like that. Why would you even ask?"

"I love the mystery. I think I could find out more about the motive. I was thinking about going up there and checking out the town."

"It's those mystery books you've been reading since you were a kid." Sarah thumbed through more outfits on the rack. "So, Digby said you could cover the story?"

"Not exactly. I'm thinking about just getting some answers on my own."

"Honey, I know you are a gifted reporter, but this is serious."

"I'll be careful, I promise. I'm just going to ask the townspeople a few questions."

"Well, if I know you, you are probably going to do it even if Digs and your mother disagree. I hope you don't lose your job."

"I'm not going to do it yet. He wants me to write a nice, safe article about the town and how they are getting back on their feet. But someone up there knows something about who set those fires."

Sarah stopped Tess as she walked towards the new dress display. She rarely wore dresses but thought it would be nice to change it up during the summer months.

"Tess, please be careful. People who do criminal things like that are very dangerous. It's not your business to go around and solve every crime."

"I get it, Mom. I want to do this for Robbie and those who need to collect their losses. I won't be involved with criminals. Come on. I gotta show you this gorgeous summer dress I want to try on."

Sarah loved her daughter very much. When Tess picked a career in reporting, she expected to see her behind a computer. She didn't imagine it to be so risky.

Tess admired the reporters on the Today show and loved to watch the daily news. When she was nine years old, her mother watched her imitating them. Later, Tess traveled to many parts of the world when there was war and chaos. To do some of her investigating, she was required to wear special gear. It was uncomfortable wearing a bullet proof vest but she enjoyed telling people she was with the press. She had been inside homeless shelters and refugee camps, talking to victims who lost everything from floods, tornadoes, and earthquakes. Getting information about the fires would be no different. She believed that if she didn't learn where it was coming from and find out how to stop it, many more victims would lose everything. Tess couldn't bear to let that happen. She worked too hard to get to where she was. "I was an intern for too long on the sidelines. I don't want to hear a repeat about the risks of reporting," she muttered to herself.

She did feel bad for her parents. They always expected the worst and were relieved when she safely arrived home. To her, each new story was an adventure, a great opportunity to prove how good she could be.

The next day, Digby was busy trying to get word down onto the presses, making sure his employees printed only what he asked. It seemed like the business was split into two parts, running the print and writing it. Reporters were born with it or they had to learn the passion. They were in the business of asking pertinent questions and getting the information they were looking for. Sadly, too many of them got lazy and made him find a replacement who had the fire it took to research and write what really counted.

"Mackey, where's Tess?" Digby yelled across the room.

"She said she's on her way."

"Let me know when she gets in."

"Sure, Digs."

Digby was looking at the email Margo sent once again. He couldn't get it out of his mind that Tess wanted to get more information first-hand. He wanted her to limit herself to the office and fill a column about victims coping with devastation. Tess walked in carrying a stack of papers.

"Hey, Tess. Digs is looking for you."

"Thanks."

She walked in while he was wrapping up a phone call.

"You wanted to see me?"

"Yeah. Let's be a little more punctual. You got me obsessing about this arson story. Have a seat."

"What about it?"

"I know I said I didn't want you to try to do this on your own. But I do want you to cover the victim's story and put it in a column. I received more letters and emails from the victims and their families." He put his hand on a brown box full of letters. "You can use these to do the story from here."

"We both know it's better to go to Julian and talk to the people who live there. It will have more of a local appeal."

"That may not be a bad idea, later. For now, write the column supporting their community and after that, we'll talk about doing some interviews. Right now, I think you could put your best effort into what's in this box and make it good."

"I have the drive to do more."

"I know. We can only do so much. I want the column done by early next week. I suggest you start now. By the way, Robbie's parents sent over a bio about the young reporter."

"I'll write it." Tess felt her heart break thinking about what she was going to read from the victims.

"Good, and who knows? Maybe it will help someone to come forward with more info," Digby said.

"Oh, here are the reports from when I went abroad. You can look them over and let me know when you want them to go to press."

"Sure thing. You're good, Tess. Get it done and there may be a promotion in your future."

Tess sighed and gave Digby a look.

"Hey, don't look so glum. I could have given this to Charlie. You should be glad you get it."

"I'm grateful. Thanks, Digs."

"Shut the door on your way out. I have a newspaper to run." Digby smiled at Tess as she left.

Sitting at her desk, she looked through the pictures of blackened houses ruined by fires over the last few months. She studied the damage wondering why anyone would do such a thing. It was only certain houses, and it left the town feeling afraid of who might be next. There were pictures of families and the couple who died. "Cheryl and Nathan James" was printed below it. Their only son inherited the property and planned to restore it as his permanent residence. Several homes and barns were burned and some were rebuilt, others not. Tess had seen the devastation on the news but she had never visited. Each of the families gave required information to authorities and insurance companies, but some obviously avoided telling the whole story. The first one started nearly a year before.

Searching the internet, her research revealed knowledge about the small town. Locals seemed to know each other better than her big town. She always jotted her notes on paper before putting them into her computer. She needed as many details as possible. As she worked, she realized that her work should be dedicated to Robbie. He worked hard on it too. Tess was known for precise coverage backed by facts. She didn't think it would go against Digby's request if she touched the fringes of investigative reporting. She would find a way to get more of the truth than he expected. Most of her day was spent writing a rough draft on what she learned. Working through the night and the next day, it looked ready for print, her article read this way:

Tess Charlton

News Reporter for The News Day

Many of our readers have heard of the heinous crimes involving arson that took place in Julian. The leftovers of burnt homes and the scent of smoke still haunts victims who to this day still wonder and ask, 'why?' Some escaped with their lives, losing everything they owned. Others lost their lives. A well-known couple paid the highest price leaving behind a puzzled son wanting answers. Working on the story, a professional and dedicated reporter, Robbie Carnes, was killed when his car went over an embankment. He was on the cusp of discovering who was involved and why. Many say it was an accident, others say he was murdered. As fellow reporters, his loss was a hard one to take. We mourned someone who was too young to die.

Why must this remain a mystery? Shouldn't this crime be solved and those causing this pain already be behind bars? The town still lives in fear and continues grieving. With all the investigations complete, the big questions are left unanswered. As any reporter, I want to get more facts and narrow down the motive. If I had the power, I would love to ease the minds of those affected. My heart goes out to the many families who worked hard to move on and build the confidence to reconstruct without further disturbance.

What is next for the town of Julian? Donations have been given to those who deserve to be made whole again. It was proven that the James home was the first to be torched. Did the arsonists know they were in the home at the time? Why were other houses

18

targeted? There has to be a reason why and we hope soon we will all know the truth about the fires in our small San Diego County town.

The article named the families and many charities that helped raise money to support victims and farmers that took pride in their town. There were pictures of the burnt barns and homes along with photos of the people affected. She thought it was good to add a byline to inspire readers to come forward:

Robbie Carnes will be remembered as a reporter who loved his job. He was kind and obsessed with getting facts. He was a lot like I was at that age. At twenty two, his life was taken away too early. Was it because he was interested in the arson or did he know something more? Robbie was among some of the victims who lost their lives over the evils that someone inflicted on innocent humans. These people must be caught. Many still hunger for the answers that provide them hope. If anyone wants to share information, your privacy is respected. Let's do our part to help this community.

Margo came over to see her again. She was like a sister to her and knew how strong willed Tess could be.

"Hey, I'm here. I'm going to make a latte and why don't you ever lock this door?" Margo asked from the kitchen.

"I'm in writing mode. Don't distract me," she replied.

Margo wanted to read what Tess wrote.

"How's it going so far?" she asked looking over her shoulder.

"So far, okay. I have a few days to complete another page or two. Do you think Digs will like it?"

"Well, I like it. You know how he can be. Something tells me you are going to do more than just write this article. I worry about you."

"Digby said I could visit the town and interview some of the people. Well, he actually said after I'm finished with this and after he approves. That seems harmless."

"I know you. You won't stop with just an interview."

"If there is more that I can do, I want to be part of it."

"Be sensible. If you did get any information, would you tell the police about it?"

"After I gather my facts, yes. I would...for Robbie."

"Tess, you're starting to become a woman who sits all alone trying to solve crimes. You should get a new hobby or a dog."

"A dog? You know I hate pets. They're dirty and they can ruin your house in minutes! Even if I did like animals, I can't take care of them. I'm never home. They would die at home."

"My point exactly."

"I hate staying home."

"Well, maybe going to Julian will help ease your mind knowing there is nothing left for you to solve."

"No, there is a motive out there somewhere. Why would someone want to burn down all those buildings and homes?"

"Wouldn't that be something if you found out more? That would put you in a good place with the paper."

"Now you see why I want to get to the bottom of it."

"When are you going to post the article?"

"As soon as I am finished."

Margo could do nothing to convince her friend to lose her risky thoughts. She just hoped that this wouldn't be her last report and she would stay safe.

After working all night on the project, Tess decided to take her chance and drive up early the next morning without telling anyone. She was tired of hearing advice to leave it alone. The obsession was too strong to hold her back. That night, she packed the pictures of the destroyed properties, knowing she was invading sensitive spaces where residents were still living in fear. She had developed sympathy for them without their knowledge and would have to approach them with ease, careful not to ask triggering questions that would make her look like a nosy reporter. They had already had their share of microphones and cameras in their face. Pictures could never tell the story like being there where the damage was done. She was prepared to see firsthand what broke the hearts of kindhearted folks who only wanted peace. Yet, someone knew something more. They had to. How could no one have a hint of why they were targeted? She didn't know how long it would take to get her facts and she didn't care. Taking her time would help people gain her trust.

Tess didn't get much sleep that night. She was up before the sun and ready to have what she called, "an adventure." This was unlike when she was in Afghanistan where she heard bombs and shots fired as she wrapped her arms around frightened people who feared living that way. Her mind was filled with stressful moments and happy times getting to know different cultures. She was glad to wear a burqa or a hijab that women wore to show respect. She wanted to blend in and when it seemed like things were grim, she made it comfortable for anyone wanting to smile. That was Tess. She wanted to make an imprinted impact on anyone who felt like life dealt them a bad hand. To her, there was always hope. Those were the thoughts she kept close to her heart.

That morning was the last straw for Tess. She wouldn't call it, "taking the law into her own hands." Her heart truly believed she could end the terror and ease the hearts of families who deserved to live life the way they wanted. Tess was prepared for most things to come her way when it came to getting facts. Her camera and recorder were her best friends. She was gifted in capturing the most amazing shots that Digby often put next to her article. Tess had a lot of confidence and was always on alert for anything that might come up, exciting or serious. Her mother never could understand what made her full of that type of energy. Tess came into her own at a young age. She would never imagine that her risks could drastically change her life. So far, she loved the ride she was on. Digby once said, "There is no one that is more dedicated than Tess. I have seen many come and go, but Tess is the queen of reporting." His belief spurred her on. Without that confidence, she may not have jumped at all the opportunities presented to her. Tess was going to do the riskiest thing she had ever done in her career.

Chapter 3

Trust Wore a Mask

It was a twisting road up to Julian. One side of the
road was littered with fallen rocks from above and the
other side was a deadly precipice. When a truck swept
past her from the other direction, she could feel her
Jeep sway. It was easy to see how so many people lost
their lives every year on that grade. She stayed on high
alert until she topped the slope and the road
straightened out.

Just before town, she found Deer Run, a dusty road to
a few homes. If her map was right, one of them was a
black pile of debris. After passing a few mailboxes, she
parked by an open gate and walked in toward the
home. There were no cars around and the grass had
grown up around the fence line. What could she find
that would lead her somewhere? The left side
sustained the most damage, probably near where the
kitchen was. The back door was kicked in and
everything smelled like soot. Her curiosity pushed her
to go inside. It was obvious that this was a historic
home. She pulled out her camera and adjusted it. A
clawfoot bathtub stood near a window. The lath was
exposed with some of the nails intact where the plaster
was falling off. Wires hung where the ceiling used to
be. Cobwebs dangled as the wind blew between the
charred cracks. The smell of burnt wood was strong
and the fine dust made it hard to breathe. It had been
sitting in that state for some time and she wondered
why it wasn't repaired. She looked out the broken
window and saw the view the home was surrounded
by. A narrow field of grass swayed back and forth by
the wind. Flowerbeds were damaged and trees were
partially burned. Tess guessed the trees would heal on

their own in good time. It was sad and shameful. She closed her eyes and thought of what it would be like to live in this house. She could envision the clothes hanging on the line as she walked barefoot through the soft, cool grass. Seeing it firsthand was heartbreaking. She had to get down to business. Maybe one of the neighbors could give more information.

No one was home at the house across the way, so she tried the place she spotted on the way in. There was no gate or fence. The windows were opened and a few dry bushes grew wild near the edge of the house. Speckled chickens were quietly pecking at the ground. She took off her ball cap and sunglasses.

"Hi! Anyone home?"

"Yeah, were back here," an elderly voice replied.

She walked around the side of the place and a man was working on an old car that had seen better days. His wife was sitting in the shade of a porch sipping iced tea. Their dog was by her side and stood up as Tess walked closer.

"Hi. I am Tess Charlton. I wanted to visit with some of the neighbors here. Is that okay?" she asked the man whose hands were greasy. As he looked at her, he wiped them with a dirty rag.

"As long as it's okay with Bessie here," he said dryly.

"That's me," the woman acknowledged. "What do you want?"

"Because of your neighbor's fires, I have been writing some things down that might help solve it. Do you know anything I might add?"

"Done told most of it to the Sheriff months ago. Are you with the authorities?"

Tess dug deeper, "No. I have a special interest in the people here. Are there any concerns you have for your community?"

"I don't see why this interests you. You obviously are not from 'round here. What's your business?"

"Well, I'm a reporter who cares."

"Reporters just want to be recognized as nosy. Besides, what good would it do to tell you a story? I suggest you git and leave it alone."

"Don't you want answers? I want to help your town."

"Sorry, young lady. No one is going to solve what is broken," the old man replied.

She looked at the man who stared at her and then he sat down by his wife. Tess didn't know what else to say. She could tell they were still saddened by their neighbor's damages. She backed up to leave.

"Thank you for your time. I'm sorry to have disturbed you."

He piped up, "Hey, we appreciate that you care."

"Thank you for that."

Tess glimpsed a look back at the couple who would never again trust anyone and gave up hope for anything better. That was why her mission was so ingrained in her. She looked out at the horizon as the wind blew an earthy smell in her face and stared back at the little house in the middle of God's country. It was a place that deserved calm and by no means forsaken.

On the other side of town, were the sights of two more damaged buildings. The first one looked like it was slowly being rebuilt. Stacks of lumber and roofing were under tarps. No one was around but footprints were found everywhere in the dust. The fields were black underneath with bright green blades filling in.

The smell was strong, as wind stirred up the ground that chose to hang on to the odor.

The second home was at the end of a lengthy drive. Dry grass covered most of the roadway and could be heard brushing up against her rig. She observed a road on the right that looked like it was used the most. After passing it, she came into full view of a brick-faced home missing it's roof. As she stepped out, she spotted heavy tire tracks, broken windows, charred two-by-fours, and an aluminum ladder lay on the ground. The doorway beckoned her inside. As she put her head in, the daylight fell between timbers casting patterns in the dust. Melted objects sat on the floor where furniture used to be. She ached thinking about what the families were going through as they saw their home burning. She touched the charred wood and stepped carefully to avoid weakened floorboards. Metal plumbing was exposed and the tub and toilet were removed. Not much was done to finish the job. It may have been because there was no more money. Where were the people who lived here? Were they staying with family or friends? Did they become homeless? She was angered at what she saw.

"Why would someone want to do this?" she wondered aloud.

As she stepped away, the noise of a truck grew louder. With large tires, it ominously bounced toward the house with a dust trail behind it. An older man got out and walked straight at her.

"What do you want here?" he asked gruffly.

"Is this your house?"

"No, but it's not yours either. I asked you, what do you want here?"

"My name is Tess and I am doing a story on the families who survived the fires. Do you have some information for me?"

"Maybe I do and maybe I don't. I don't know you from Adam. You could be anyone. You have some ID?"

Tess pulled out a reporter's ID lanyard and handed it to him.

"If I remember anything, I'll give it to the law. But tell me, just what are you looking for that they couldn't already find?"

"Well, that is what I was hoping you could fill in for me. I want to get answers as much as you do."

He looked at her card more closely and added, "You really should not be out here all alone like this. Better for you to head back down into the valley where it's safe. This is not the kind of place for a city girl." He handed her card back to her.

Tess began to feel a bit nervous. His face revealed he knew more than he let on.

"I understand. All I want to do is help. Do you believe someone will fix this place up, bringing it back to normal?"

"No. I don't believe in miracles. The person who did this is still out there. You are one small person. There's no way an outsider can help. I'm sorry, I need to get back and you need to leave, and don't come back here! It's not for the likes of you."

"Okay, I'll leave. Before I go, whose house is this?"

"Let's just say, someone who misses the life they used to have."

"I really am sorry for this loss."

She turned and climbed back into her Jeep and drove back to the main road. She believed that the home belonged to the man she talked to. After waiting another ten minutes at the end of the road, she noted that he would not follow her out and she continued her search for the other homes. Not forgetting the gruff stranger, she decided it was better to head into town to see if the café was open. Looking at those homes filled her with pain and the images were not going to leave her mind. She needed to focus. That meant not calling her mother or Margo nor accepting any calls for a while. After she entered the café, her cell phone rang and then hung up. She ordered a slice of apple pie and coffee and then a text appeared.

"Tess Charlton, the reporter looking for info about the fires?"

Even if it was outside of her plan, she was going to respond to it.

"Yes. Who is this?"

"A neighbor of one of the homes you are investigating. No one ever asked me what I know, but I think it might be helpful if I give my input."

"I am at the Julian café and bakery. Do you want to meet me here?"

"Give me fifteen minutes."

At six o'clock, she received another text that he was parked outside in a silver Bronco. She swallowed her last bit of coffee and grabbed her purse.

"Hello. I am Daniel Masters." He was wearing sunglasses.

"Yes. How did you get my number?"

"I called the paper."

"So, you have evidence for me, Mr. Masters?"

"Please, call me Dan. I'm very familiar with this area."

"Do you live here?" she inquired.

"I used to. These folks are pretty quiet when it comes to anything about the fires."

"I'm finding that out. They still seem scared."

"I've read your columns. You are a good reporter."

"I worked hard to get to where I'm at. Are you well known in the town? I mean, are you friends with anyone here?"

"Not too many. A few of them don't like that I want to bring a little bit of the city to Julian."

"What do you mean?"

Let's just say, I have a lot to bring to the table."

"Maybe the neighbors don't want you to citify their home. Is that what you want to do?"

"Only a little bit. This place just needs some help."

"Let's get back to what you may have for my report. What do you have to share with me?" Tess circled back.

"I don't want to spill it to the whole world. You know what I mean?"

"Not really. I think the public deserves to know."

"If it solves anything, the authorities will pay me quite a bit, sort of a reward. But, for you and your paper, it has to be worth something. Tell me, what's in it for me?" he asked.

"I'm not doing this for the money. The paper doesn't pay anyone for a story. Are you saying you want to make a difference or is this about a payoff?"

"Of course. I want to do something for the community. This is a good group of people here. They deserve better. That's the right answer."

He tilted his handsome face slightly and looked into her eyes. He looked sincere. He expressed the same feelings she had for the town. She briefly thought that he would be good for an undiscovered lead.

As she put her pen to paper, he flirtingly reached out and touched her hand, gently putting it down to stop her.

"Dan, what is it you want from me? I have to get the real facts. "

He looked around to see if anyone was in earshot. Quietly he admitted, "I saw a red truck."

"Is this about the person who was driving the truck?"

"It was dusk. I couldn't see a face, but the truck was seen around where the last home burned down."

"Why were you there?"

"I have a place nearby."

"Why didn't you go to the police?"

"I had no evidence to prove anything. I have been the upstanding citizen who has been offering these people money to buy their properties and help rebuild. Of course, they all turned me down. I guess I just wanted a chance to make the town better."

She was wrapped up in the sound of his voice. He sounded like a humanitarian with social experience. He played with his fingers and leaned a little closer to give her inside information.

"There are only two trucks built like that around here and the evening of the fire. I saw the old red truck. It is the kind with those two round headlights mounted close together. Unmistakably, I saw them flickering down the road that night, you know, bouncing. I didn't think anything much about it until the next morning when smoke wafted near where I lived. Something was wrong. Later in the day, a Sheriff's SUV went by and asked me a couple of questions. But no one wants a Sheriff in their business, so I just told him nothing. Was that wrong?"

"I don't know. I would have said something. I'm hoping to get more evidence compiled and ready to email it tonight. I can add this to it."

"You are very thorough with your findings, aren't you?"

"I'd like to think that I am extremely professional."

"I can see that," he conceded. His eyes studied her face.

Before she finished writing, she added, "You said there were only two of those trucks around. What do you mean?"

"Oh that. Well, Cooper has one he is rebuilding in his yard. The other one belongs to a homestead near Mountain View. I don't remember their name, though. Do you think this is important?"

Tess was taking notes as quickly as she could and paused to look at him. "Are you saying that you think they had something to do with the fires? I deal with facts. We can't just speculate and I need a motive. What happened to these people was extreme, maybe traumatizing."

He looked up toward the pale moon sliding up over the horizon and said to her, "Mountain View has those two dirt roads. Is it the first road that have the moonshiners with shotguns? Don't ever get caught at the wrong one. I got caught in that place one time."

He looked at Tess seriously, "You shouldn't go up there by yourself to check it out."

"I have been through worse situations. I'm not afraid to go."

"No, no, a lot of people wind up missing up there. I could go up there alone, but I don't ask the right questions like you professionals do," he paused. He was trying to be concerned about her safety.

"And that truck was there when the fires started?"

"No way to find out unless we check it out."

Tess blurted out almost too quickly, "Take me up there! It's not quite dark yet. Just let me get a good look at the place and if it looks unsafe tonight, I can come back tomorrow."

"You sure? Okay, let's do this." He hesitated and then walked to his car. He took a quick glance across his shoulder before he climbed in confidently.

She attached her seatbelt, "I'm looking for a breakthrough. If it's not worth it, I'll have to try another way to get my story."

As they turned North to go over the mountain road toward Palomar, she asked him about his job and how long he lived around Julian. He gave vague answers, saying he was in real estate and had always wanted to make the town better, but he had to get some neighbors on his side. He then added questions of his own. It was quiet for ten minutes until he spoke again.

"So, Tess, what have you got so far? How long are you going to keep investigating something that may or may not surface?"

"As long as it takes. I'm sick of it just hanging in the air when there has to be a reason."

"You think it was arson? It looked intentional from what the news said. Even law enforcement could only guess. What more have you found if I can be so bold? If you haven't already noticed, I want to help and be part of this with you."

"Well, I thank you for this lead. But I can do the rest myself. That's my job."

"I would like to help out with your other clues too."

"That's okay. Why are you going out of your way to help me, Dan?"

"Maybe it's because of this story or that you are very fascinating."

"Let's keep this professional." She was uncomfortable with his verbiage."

"Fair enough." He threw his hands in the air and looked away from her face.

"What is your full reason? I'm a good listener. You said you have been where the moonshiners are. Why were you there if it was dangerous?"

"Just searching for property. When it comes to these people up here, it's better for a man with experience to face them than a pretty girl like yourself."

She looked at him with confusion. Her instincts with previous informants raised a red flag when something wasn't quite right. His answers seemed very indirect. Why did it feel like a sycophant using flattery to influence her? He was looking straight ahead while Tess searched from her window, frantically looking for signs of their destination.

"You seem anxious. No need to worry. We're getting close. It's up here on the right," he appeased.

"I think you should let me out right here," she asked nervously trying to keep her composure.

Something in his tone made her heart race. She was hoping the Mountain View sign would appear as soon as possible. He turned his headlights on as the last of the sunset fell to the west. It had been about thirty minutes since they left town. He finally turned right onto a gravel road. Where was the sign? Did they miss it?

He broke the silence again. "This was what you wanted. Have you changed your mind?"

"Where are you taking me?" she asked calmly.

The glow of the dashboard lights revealed a stressed face and his jaw seemed clinched.

Tess realized there was trouble. It was the sort of thing Digs and her mother warned her about. Dan's driving was faster and more erratic.

"Don't panic," she told herself in her head.

When under pressure, her father always said, "Be bold, assertive, and stronger than your opponent."

"Stop!" she yelled. "Stop right here and let me out!"

"Sorry, Tess. I can't do that. You see, you're a busybody and you know too much. I can't let you go to the press with this. Didn't anyone ever tell you not to trust a stranger?" His eyes stayed focused on the road.

"You had something to do with the fires, didn't you?"

"You're not only beautiful, but you're also smart."

"Where are you taking me?" she repeated.

"Someplace they can't find you," he smirked.

Tess had to do something to stop the car. She needed to find a way to get out of the danger. Was Dan part of the fires or an accomplice? She had to act quickly. Her life depended on it. She glanced at the keys and Dan picked up on what she was thinking and put his hand out.

"Oh, no. Don't get any ideas about taking the keys." He grabbed her wrist aggressively.

She used it as a distraction before she acted on a thought that crossed her mind. It was frightening, but she had to save her own life.

As Dan turned the corner, she shouted, "You are not going to take me anywhere!"

She jerked the steering wheel toward her and the SUV veered to the right enough to scare him. He overcompensated by turning the wheel in the opposite direction. The vehicle was suddenly broadside and began to roll until it reached the edge. Both of their heads bounced against the headliner, the window and then the door panel. The inertia continued over the shoulder and landed six feet onto a small tree and rolled another twenty feet to smash against a boulder. The grinding and twisting of metal ended. The motor died. Two people lay unconscious as one of the tires finished spinning.

Chapter 4

Who Was She?

Tess had thoughts of colorful blurs and swirls coming in and out of focus. She felt relaxed, as if she was hallucinating. It was time to wake up as she forced her eyes to open. Her neck was a little stiff and her eyelids fluttered in an attempt to awaken. It was definitely morning, but it was still dark. Tess moved her left hand to rub her eyes but her right arm wouldn't move. A belt was holding her down. She was locked in a seatbelt. She reached down and unclipped it and her body fell a few inches. She adjusted her eyes to her surroundings. Why was the car on its side? She reached for the door handle but it was locked shut. The door had been crushed. The airbags were deployed. Was the window open or broken? Her mind finally realized she was in a car accident. Next to her, was a man that looked unfamiliar. He wasn't moving. He was face down onto the steering wheel. She didn't think about checking to find out if he was alive. Instinctively, she crawled through the car window, moaning and feeling pain course throughout her body. Squeezing her way out of the mangled car, she stood up, wobbling and unbalanced. Her world spun in circles. Every part of her body began to feel the aching and she felt the urge to stretch. She attempted to shake out shards of glass from her hair and screamed in pain, falling to the ground. She crawled away from the wreck, trying not to get sick from the pain in her head. A sickening feeling came over her and she bent over into a bush and threw up. The nausea was evident and she needed a place to rest until it subsided. The man was still unconscious. She could feel her bruises. Where was she? Why was this man with her? She speculated that he was someone she should escape from before he woke up. She did not know why she felt afraid. What caused this wreck? Was he dead? She was asking all kinds of questions and came up with no answers. Her instincts told her that she needed to get away despite the pain she felt when she walked. The urge to leave intensified. She didn't think to look around or search for anything. She just wanted to get away from the scene. The trees scared her and it was difficult to walk on the ground that was covered in twigs and pine needles. She looked up and suddenly got sick again. It was very hard to see since her sight was being compromised from the blow to her head.

By moonlight, her eyesight adjusted to see a trail leading down across the hillside. Maybe that was the way out to wherever she was going. She pulled her hoody over her head to warm up and began the journey to somewhere. She was going to have to spend the night hiking in the near darkness. After a few hours, she reached a mossy piece of ground under some Alder trees. Lying down, she was riddled with frustrated wonderment, settling deep into the forest. She needed to sleep and for about four hours, she rested being awoke with noises stirring in the night occasionally. Sleeping in the middle of nowhere was terrifying. She had nothing to keep her warm or no one to talk to about the crash. She would fall back to sleep with thoughts rolling in and out of her head trying to make sense of her surroundings. When she saw daylight, she recalled climbing out of a car to get away from an unknown man. Not knowing if he was dead or alive, she didn't want to be linked to a possible crime. She had to take care of herself. Nothing was clear in her mind. She looked back at the trail she came from. She remembered the man, the hike and nothing else. Where did it all go? Her clothes were slightly dirty and she had pain finding its way through every muscle as she slowly walked the trail downhill toward the sunrise.

"What is wrong with me? I know who I am and what to do." She furrowed her brow, "I am... Oh, this is crazy! I know who I am. It makes no sense," she continued muttering to herself. She was frustrated trying to gather any memory of who she was.

She reached down and drank a handful of water from the stream. The nausea returned and she couldn't think about food right now. She splashed its coolness onto her face. When she touched her forehead, she cried out, feeling the pain of a burning gash. She bent down and washed the blood off. Her head ached and she realized she was hungry. A few more handfuls and she continued wearily. She didn't want to walk any further but she knew she had to find a way out of the forest and possibly get help. The air was getting colder and clouds darkened the trail.

After three more hours of following the narrow path, she finally heard traffic on a small road below her. In between those hours, she had to find time to rest. She paused before stepping out into the open. For the time, maybe it was best to stay near the edge of the forest. She didn't feel completely safe. She had no clue who she was or why she was in her situation. It was scaring her and the best thing she could think of was to talk to no one until it was figured out. The air was filled with the smell of nitrogen as large raindrops began to fall, each one creating a tiny dust cloud.

The road forked to the left and at the corner sat a large barn with a sign that read, FEED STORE on the building. The parking area was vacant and under the eaves looked like a good place to rest. She walked around to the front of the store and retrieved a newspaper from a garbage can near the door. After reading the date and location, she started to cry. Fear filled her and all she thought about was getting back to who she was. Nothing led her to know any more than before. The nature of this place was weird, the date was odd and she still did not have a name to place on herself. In desperation, she thumbed through the newspaper, looking for something she could remember or for the time being, to call herself. In bold letters, under wedding announcements, she saw the names, "Ryan and Lauren to be wed today."

"Okay. Ryan Lauren. That's okay with me. I'm Ryan," she kept affirming.

She felt it was still not right, it wasn't really her. It was a different person; someone she didn't recognize. Even her speech sounded strange and she definitely didn't want anyone to notice.

Looking at a bulletin board outside of the store, she noticed posted ads. The one written on lined paper attracted her attention. She pulled it off the pin and read it.

Hired hand wanted. Full time job taking care of my farm animals and feeding. Room and board included. Inquire at 1122 Old Valley Road. Ask for Marion Jones

Tess was intrigued. To hide away where no one knew her or would question any information about her, would give her time to become herself again, whoever that was. The last thing she wanted was someone asking questions she couldn't answer. With the ad in her hand, she went inside where she could talk to the clerk. She pulled her hoodie over her head to hide her injury. She looked down as she talked to the clerk.

"Excuse me. Do you know this person?"

"Oh, yeah. Marion's known for her goat and animal farm. You looking for a job?" The boy tried to get a better look at her face.

"Yes. Where is this address?" It was hard to get the words out, even to ask a question. She felt heavily drugged.

"If you wait a few minutes, I can take you there. It's just up the road about thirty miles on the way to my next delivery. Let me get someone to cover for me."

"Thank you."

He shouted to someone in the back, "Hey, Davey, I'm going to give this young lady a ride to Marion's place and then deliver the feed to Jack's. I'll be back in an hour."

"Okay."

Tess was looking at the pastries displayed near the coffee. She was hungry, but still not feeling well enough to eat.

"Would you like a donut? You look kinda hungry."

"I can't eat anything at the moment."

"When you get to Marion's, she can fix you something if you change your mind. She's a good cook."

She asked to use the restroom to clean up. It would create fewer questions. She climbed in the truck and tried not to say much of anything. She was still in shock over what happened and just wanted to find someplace to rest. Her eyes closed until a bump in the road woke her thirty minutes later. The rain had stopped. The driveway was long and bumpy. A barbed wire fence bordered one side woven with long grasses powdered with dust the color of the road. At its end, stood an array of buildings and trees.

"Here we are. Marion Farm."

Tess slowly got out and shut the door.

"Thanks."

"Just walk up to the door. She'll take care of you."

Tess walked up the stairs the large porch and knocked on a door with oval glass. The decking on the porch was old and looked as though it was partially repaired. There were two rocking chairs and a small table on the left side and a swinging bench on the right. Tess looked around the place trying to familiarize herself with the surroundings that she might temporarily use for a home. While she was waiting, an Australian sheep dog walked up beside her and sniffed. The dog lifted his nose into her hand and she naturally petted it. The screen door opened and creaked as a woman came out. Tess tried to hide what she was going through. She felt like she just woke up from a nightmare and found it hard to remember basic things. She was taking a risk staying with a stranger until she felt better. She had no expectations when that would be.

"May I help you?" Marion asked wiping her hands on her apron.

"Yes. I'm here to answer your ad. Is the job still available?" Tess showed Marion the ad she took from the store.

"Well, yes, it is. Do you know what this job entails? You look like a tiny little thing."

"I think I can do whatever you ask me to do."

"I was expecting a strapping young man with hard work in him to help me out. I've never seen you around here. Where are you from?"

Tess could feel her heart beating wildly. What kind of answer would not give herself away?

"I'm from the city. I thought a change would be good."

"A city girl? Well, you definitely came to a place that is different. You look innocent enough and could use a good meal. Do you have any bags?"

"Uh, no, no bags. Just me."

"Did Travis drive you here? That looked like his truck."

"Yes." Tess never knew the young man's name.

"He's a good kid, just got his license this year. If he trusts you, then I guess I could give you a try for a few days. Come on in. I got some food on the stove."

It was relieving to know Tess found a place to rest and a meal to give her strength for the day. She was still trying to make sense of everything that occurred. Looking around the house, she waited, hoping she would get back her appetite. It was a typical farmhouse, but to Tess, it looked like a cozy and safe place to rest.

"After we eat, I can show you around. You get a room to yourself. Oh, by the way, what's your name?"

"Ryan. Um, Ryan Lauren."

"Well, nice to meet you, Ryan. Quite an unusual name for a woman."

"I guess so."

Tess sat at the table and smelled the aroma of food cooking in the kitchen. Hot buttered biscuits and gravy with scrambled eggs and bacon. The warm smell of brewed coffee gave the house a comfortable feel.

"Never too late in the day for a breakfast. These eggs are fresh from my hens and everything we eat is from the garden out there. I live too far out to go to those fancy supermarkets."

"There's a lot of food here for just the two of us," Tess said.

"Oh, sometimes Kyle comes over to look over my animals and he eats with me. I swear, I think that boy has a hollow belly. He can eat more than my hogs."

"Kyle?" Tess asked.

"Oh, he's the town veterinarian. I was expecting him to be here today. He may be running late."

Unwittingly, Tess pulled back her hood on her sweatshirt revealing her injury. Marion noticed.

"Well, gosh almighty! What happened to you? Should I call the doctor?"

"No, I'm fine. I was hiking and fell."

"I got just the thing for that gouge. It looks like you got a bruise swelling up too. I can clean it up with some peroxide."

"Thank you."

"Sure is strange that you just walked off the earth and stumbled across this place. One thing we need to do is get you to not be so quiet. Are you a shy girl?"

"I don't think I am. I'm just getting to know the place."

"There is so much to do. I won't make you chase the greasy pigs out of the gate at first."

"What does that mean?" Tess asked confused.

"It's my way of saying, I won't work you too hard on your first week. My, you city folks! You need to lighten up a little. Old Marion knows just how to get you to open up."

Marion brought over the coffee. She wanted to get to know Tess better. She sat the coffee cup next to Tess's plate.

"How do you take your coffee?"

"Uh, just like that."

"Black?"

"Yeah, black." Tess acted like she knew what black coffee tasted like. She sipped it and immediately made a face, pushing the cup away.

"What's wrong? Too strong for ya?"

"Uh, no. I don't think I like coffee. Can I have some water?"

"Okay," puzzled Marion.

"I'm sure your coffee is fine. I hope I didn't hurt your feelings."

"You could have fooled me. You can serve yourself; glasses are on that shelf there. I'll be right back."

Marion noticed road dust outside the window. A white SUV drove up to the house. It was the Sheriff. He lived across the valley and kept an eye on his neighbors.

"Dale, what are you doing here?"

"I was on my way to Julian and wanted to check up with you. I just heard that they found an abandoned car turned over in Caspian's forest. I'm just making the rounds to see if anyone knows about it."

"No, I haven't heard anything. I was actually looking out for Kyle."

"Well, if you hear anything, let us know."

"Will do."

Minutes later, Kyle drove up with dust busting behind his rusted pickup. The bed was full of cages, chicken feed, and a sign on the passenger door: Kyle James, Veterinarian DVM. Marion was just about to go back into the house but instead came down the porch stairs to greet him.

"Well, right on time. I got some breakfast waiting for you in the kitchen. Get yourself in here."

"Thanks. How's old Coot doing?"

"Better. The infection has cleared up. You can go out and see him after you eat."

"That's why I'm here, and for your irresistible cooking."

"Kyle, the bottomless pit."

He came into the house and noticed someone sitting at the table.

"Hello," he said to Tess with her back to him. "Marion, who's your guest?"

"This is Ryan. She's my new hired hand."

"Really? She's knee high to a pond frog."

"Excuse me?" Tess turned her body toward him.

"What. Are you hard of hearing? Those hands look too delicate for a shovel."

"Kyle, be nice to Ryan. She just needs a chance to prove she can do the job."

"I don't need to be judged by some cowboy."

"Cowboy? That's probably a compliment."

"I didn't mean it to be."

"Well, look at that! She's standing up for herself. I told her to toughen up and she's listening," Marion declared.

"She doesn't look so tough."

"I just might surprise you!" Tess was tired of his sarcasm.

"Come on, you two," Marion said as she passed a plate to Kyle.

"So where did you come from? I've never seen you around here," Kyle began.

"Ryan is from the city. She just wants to fit into our small town."

"There isn't much to tell. I just wanted a chance to try out the country." She was sipping her water looking at the kitchen sink.

"Interesting," Kyle finished.

Marion spoke as she brought the butter to the table. "Ryan, I'll show you some of the animals on this farm. They are just the most gentle creatures. They are like my family."

"Did Dave call you about the order of alfalfa he was delivering?" Kyle interrupted.

"No. I must have been outside when he called."

"She doesn't own a cell phone," Kyle mentioned to Tess.

"Why do I need one? I wouldn't even know how to use the darn thing."

"Dave let me know he will be delayed until tomorrow."

"I'm sure I have enough until then."

"Ryan, Kyle is here quite a bit, so you will have plenty of time to get to know him. He can teach you how to feed the animals."

"It would be my pleasure to help Ryan with her chores," he said as he brought the coffee cup to his lips.

"I don't think I need any help."

"Oh, yes you will," Kyle blurted.

Tess looked annoyed. She had to make the best of what was given. She knew nothing about taking care of animals.

"Why don't you show her where we keep the critters? I'm sure she would like to get to know them since she will be feeding them."

"That won't be necessary."

"Nonsense. Kyle, take Ryan out to the barn. Give her the tour."

"Anything for you, Marion."

Tess walked out through the backdoor and was amazed at the beauty of the place. It just felt right. She breathed in deeply and liked the smell that reached her. Watching the wind playing with the tall grass, the open meadow seemed to call her. Studying the horizon, it was like nothing she had ever seen. Walking toward the wood barn, she smiled seeing how the animals were well cared for.

"Well, what do you think? Do you think you can handle all of this?" Kyle asked her.

"How hard is it to feed a pig? You just give them hay."

"Pigs don't eat hay. They eat slop. You know, leftovers of vegetables, fruits, and grain. That pig there is Coot, he's the oldest. He got his leg caught in a wire fence last week and it got nasty. It's hard to keep the hogs out of the mud since they love it so much."

"He seems to be okay now."

"He's doing better. Do you like horses?"

"Sure. Does Marion have horses?"

"Oh, yeah. This is a well-known farm. Marion dedicated herself to her animals after her husband died. He was the one who took care of them and I guess, she wanted to carry on his legacy. She has only the two horses now." He was curious about Tess's backstory. Besides the cut on her forehead, she was pretty to look at and he sensed some mystery.

"So, what did you do in the city before you came here?" Kyle asked intriguingly.

"I...I don't think it makes a difference to know that much about me. I want to live in the present, right now. Having this job is important to me."

"Well, okay. Your hands look too perfect to be a hired hand. Be sure to use the gloves, hard work will tear them up. Marion is, well she's like my mother. She took care of me after my parents died."

"I'm sorry. How long ago?"

"Close to a year. I've been slowly rebuilding the house after the fire and I stay up there when I'm not treating patients." He was uncomfortable and walked away to curb his anxiety.

"Kyle, just to let you know, I won't hurt or betray Marion. She is very likeable," she affirmed.

"She's been through a lot in her life. I just want to be there for her and I hope you do the same."

"I will try."

"C'mon. Let's go see the horses. I'll show you where she keeps the feed."

He opened the hasp to a flimsy door where the tack hung. Bags of grain sat against the wall and Tess looked at the leather straps and polished metal that dangled from hooks.

"Two scoops of grain in the morning with their alfalfa. Just pour it in their stall bucket."

"I've never smelled anything like this before."

"That's a farm for you."

He scooped out a little grain into his hand and closed the door. She followed him toward the mare, who trotted over as she nuzzled him and quickly nibbled the grain from his hand. She watched Kyle caress her with the other hand while complimenting her with his soothing tone. Tess walked nearer and the horse stepped forward. Her hand extended to touch the mare's nose. Kyle watched how she reacted near the animal. As a skilled veterinarian, he had a keen eye for reading body language. She seemed a little timid and wary, but not fearful.

He stared at her for a moment. He was feeling protective of Marion and when this stranger came into her life, he questioned, "Who is this person?"

She noticed him staring.

"What? Why are you looking at me that way? How can you be so annoying and gentle at the same time?" Tess asked quizzically.

"What do you mean? I'm not annoying. I think you're just not used to cowboys who love animals."

Tess just smirked and decided not to respond.

"So, what's the name of this horse?" she asked.

"Her name is Maisie. That one over there is Dalton. He is the gentlest," he answered as he watched her facial expression.

"I just haven't been around animals much. I want a chance to learn more about them."

"Is that why you came here, to learn about them?"

"I came here to make a change. I like the scenery."

"There is more to this life than just scenery."

"I know that. If you're going to be here a lot, maybe you could give me time to prove how capable I am. Just because I am a woman doesn't mean I'm weak." She crossed her arms.

"I'm sorry. I know a lot of strong women out this way. You might be one of them." He sighed still having thoughts about the stranger he just met. "I should check out old Coot and get back to my clinic."

"I guess you should."

As she watched him walk back to his truck, she thought about what he said. It was going to be challenging and hopefully, rewarding. She had to be careful about being found out without it hurting Marion.

Tess needed to create a new world for herself and take on the life of someone she never knew. The first night in Marion's home, she did not sleep well. The windows were always left opened and farm animal sounds constantly interrupted her thoughts. How could she make up a person and hide who she might have been? Of course, there was no memory of her past. She knew no other way to get by until she could remember what happened to her. She was not living a lie. She wasn't sure who the man in the car was or why she was with him. She wondered if she had parents, friends, or anyone close to her who lived near.

As she finally drifted off to sleep, Tess had a dream about the face she vaguely remembered from the car. She could see him mumbling sounds of his name. She sat up terrified. Tess was suffering from amnesia from the accident. Unsure when her memory would return, somebody must be looking for her. In the meantime, she must stay safe at the farm.

The next morning, Marion was heard walking up the steps to the house. The screen door slammed.

"These are for you," Marion announced. She purchased some boots, shirts, and jeans. "Hope these are your size. I used to be that size once. Oh, that was too many years ago."

"Oh, thank you. That is very nice of you."

"A girl with no clothes; odd if you ask me. But there you go. Use the boots when you feed the animals. The muck and manure can ruin good shoes."

Just then, they both heard the sound of gravel as Kyle pulled in. Tess wasn't completely comfortable around him. Marion knew it was for a good reason.

"Hey, Ryan, are you ready to do some work?" Marion asked.

"Why is he here?" Tess asked sarcastically.

"He's here to help you out. He knows a lot about this farm and he's a vet. You could learn a lot from him, so listen close. Start by cleaning out the stalls. I'll call you when lunch is ready."

"Come on," he said, guiding her to the barn.

Tess plodded behind Kyle, unsure of what was in store for her. Inside, hanging on the wall, were all sorts of metal tools. He pulled a couple of them down.

"Here, take this rake."

"What do you want me to do with it?"

"Rake out the manure from the horse stalls."

"Ew, where do I put it?"

"We pile it in that wheelbarrow and dump it out by the garden over there. She uses it for fertilizer and what we don't use, she trades. We reuse everything here. I got you some good leather gloves. Here, you're going to need them."

Tess put on the gloves and tried to use the rake the best she knew how. She was still displaying symptoms of weakness from her ordeal. Kyle watched as she attempted to work the rake like a child.

"No, dig, dig in there. Like this. Pull it into a pile and then you can shovel it into the wheelbarrow." Kyle was patiently trying to guide her through it.

Tess stopped and felt uneasy with the word, "dig." It reminded her of something. She stopped and stared looking away from Kyle. She turned toward him squinting her eyes as she spoke. "Why did she ask you to help me?"

"She didn't ask me to come, I wanted to be here."

"Why?"

"I've always taken care of Marion. Even before my parents died, I was coming here to lend a hand. Her husband, Jeb, was a good friend to my family and the community. When he got sick, Marion just wasn't the same. Everyone came together to support her and she got better, until the fires happened."

"Fires? What fires?"

"I would think since you were from the city, you would have known about some of the fires nearby. About fifty miles over, there were several homes destroyed and a few barns. Some of them were historical, over a hundred years old. My parents died inside one of those blazes."

"I am so sorry. Did they find out who did it?"

"No. We all just gave up looking. I think my parents were asleep when it engulfed their home. They couldn't make it out in time." He paused and looked down.

After wiping his eyes with his sleeve, he reached around the stall to grab a shovel.

"Scoop like this. Don't get too much or it will hurt your back. Give your muscles some time to get used to it. Its hard work, but it builds character, that's what my dad always said. I can help you with this for an hour and then I have to get back to my office. I have a few animals needing care today."

Tess hoped she would like this kind of work. He was right, her muscles were not used to labor. Her body only allowed her to work for a short time. When Kyle left the barn, he saw Marion outside of the henhouse looking over at the two of them. Something felt wrong and he walked over to talk to her.

"Don't you think it's weird that this girl is here? It seems like she is lost and doesn't know how to do much of anything," Kyle inferred.

"Maybe there's a reason she's here. I think she needs the hard work. Remember, different doesn't mean incapable. Let's see where it takes her. Who knows, she may need us to help her through this stage in her life."

"I don't know. It's like she's hiding something."

"Oh, now you'll drive yourself crazy trying to figure her out, or any woman for that matter."

Kyle listened. He looked back toward the stables and felt some empathy. He shouldn't have judged Tess so harshly or quickly. He wanted to make things right with her. If he was going to be here often, he needed to get along with this woman.

"Be right back, Marion," he paused.

He walked back over to the barn and watched her for a few seconds.

"How's it going?" he asked.

"I think I'm getting the hang of it. I'm not myself today, so I'm sorry if it's not done right."

"You are doing great for a first day. Listen, Ryan. I want to also apologize for being unkind. I'm a little on edge since so many reporters and Sheriffs have been asking a lot of questions lately. I've been kind of leery when it comes to new people."

Suddenly the word, "reporter" repeated itself in her head as of importance. She straightened up and stretched her back. "I'm harmless and being here feels good. I'm not trying to take anything away from you or Marion."

"Do you mind if I hang out for a while?"

"Sure. Do you think I can learn to ride a horse, you know, sometime?"

"Dalton's still young and Marion just got him broke. She said he's the calmest of any. He's a good one to learn on."

Kyle helped with the heavy work load. Afterwards, she went to pet the goats. The way the light reflected into the barn and onto her face looked beautiful. It put Kyle into a momentary trance. He shook his head to clear his thoughts and whistled for Dalton to saddle him up. He got on and then helped her sit behind him.

"Are you comfortable?" he asked.

"A little. It's a bit uncomfortable on the backside."

"You can hold on to my waist. I'll get him to go slow."

They rode near the edge of the wheat fields that made a rustling sound. Kyle was taking the ride gently, making sure Tess didn't get scared or fall off.

"Can I ask you something?"

"Sure," he answered.

"Is it hard missing your parents?"

"I'm getting better with it. My father was friendly with everyone he met. I'm not sure why anyone would choose our house. I don't think he had any enemies. Folks around here never hurt anyone. I just gave up finding reasons."

"I'm glad you have Marion."

"She's getting older. I have been getting busier lately. It was my idea to hire someone to help her out. I never thought someone like you would answer the ad."

"It is hard trying something new, but I'm enjoying it. I'm afraid my work quality won't be as good as it should be. I'm slow at learning new things."

"Patience is a virtue, so they say. Just pace yourself and you'll do fine."

Tess couldn't help but put her head on Kyle's back. This was a woman who needed comfort and she sensed he did too. Kyle experienced comfort feeling her lean on him as Dalton rocked them gently. Maybe there was something special about this woman who was becoming less of a stranger and more of a friend. As they returned, Marion watched from the shade of the deck, holding a dish towel and smiling. She knew she was getting older and Kyle could use a friend like Tess. She could see a spark growing. He helped her get off the horse and then examined her scar touching it gently. She cringed for a second from the ache. There was a new gleam in his eyes. He wouldn't admit it yet.

"That bruise looks painful. I hope it heals up soon."

"It doesn't hurt as much."

"Losing someone can be a lot like that bruise. Somehow, you just have to carry on and let it heal naturally."

"I believe that." She looked at his face and then came out of her stare.

He concluded, "I gotta go, Ryan. Will you take Dalton back into the barn and brush him?"

"Yes, will you be back tomorrow?"

"I have to work all day tomorrow. I'll be back soon."

He walked by the porch half-dazed.

"How was the ride?" Marion quizzed.

"It was good. Dalton took it slow."

"I love that horse; I think he's my favorite. And what do you think of Ryan? Have you changed how you feel about her working here?"

"She'll do fine. I think she is perfect. See you in two days."

55

Marion smiled with a glimmer in her aging eyes.

Kyle got into his truck and gazed back toward Tess leading Dalton to the barn. He wanted to know more about her. Her presence was still an intriguing mystery. To him, she was a woman who was new to farm life and just about everything.

Tess, unknown to herself, was a well-educated woman with hard work and sacrifice as part of her resume. The mental block she was experiencing refused to expose the strong woman she really was. What would farm life teach her about herself? More than she expected.

Chapter 5

A Man Called Dan Masters

In the moonlight, there was new movement inside the twisted Bronco. Laying in the driver's seat alone, Dan Masters was alive. The airbags saved him from death when his SUV lost control. Opening his eyes, he looked around for Tess, who was in the passenger seat. Surprisingly, she was gone. With his leg pinned, he painfully forced his way out. Through the busted out windows, he could see Tess's bag thrown from the wreckage. He crouched to open it. Inside was her wallet, lanyard, and her dead cell phone. Dan's phone was still in his pocket. Without cell service, he was not able to call his friend to pick him up. His leg was badly bruised and still bleeding from being hit by the door when the car was thrown. He was unaware how long he was unconscious. "She is either still alive or out there in the woods bleeding to death," he said to himself. Standing up, he stuffed the contents in his coat pockets and threw the bag into the canyon. Dan couldn't let anyone see him with it or in his injured state. It would be very incriminating. He was physically worse off than Tess and if anyone was in the area, he would be found out. Leaving the wreckage behind and skirting the roadside, Dan limped out of the forest alongside the ditch. He finally reached a bar of cell service. He wasn't going to go into town. He called his friend who lived outside of Julian to pick him up.

"Jess, where are you?" Dan groaned.

"I'm at my home. What's going on? Did you talk to that woman yet?"

"Yes. She caused a stupid accident and the car got wrecked! I'm in bad shape. I need you to pick me up." It was hard for him to talk since he was in so much pain.

"Is she dead?"

"I don't know for sure. She was gone when I came to. I got her stuff. That could provide some valuable information. I have no idea where she is, but if she gets this out, she will ruin us."

"Does she know about you?"

"I think she does. Look, pick me up. I'm up at Caspian's forest. I'll come out where you can see me near the old road."

"Got it."

Dan Masters was a devious man who pressured townspeople into selling their land below value. It was always presented as good for the town. His pitch worked in another small town. After their deal was done, they had to leave rather quickly. The Julian town council met with Dan two years ago and asked him to cease and desist contacting families. When Dan saw the property behind Nathan's, he saw green. It was eighty acres with water and highway access that he could make a lot of money on. He would find out-of-state investors to put up money for a novel town improvement for tourists that looked highly profitable and then disappear with the funds. Before Dan could sign, Nathan quietly purchased the land. That made him furious. He felt like Nathan bought it to spite him. He believed it was promised to him and he was going to get revenge. Dan was angered that people would turn against him and they humiliated him in front of the council. It felt like all of Julian was against his plans. That property was his last chance to get rich in that county. Because Nathan took it from him, he had words with him at his home. Dan threatened and tried to intimidate him into getting what he wanted. Nathan did not back down and sent Dan away, hoping the enraged man would disappear. The next day, their home was burned down with Nathan and his wife inside. After that, other homes were destroyed and no one knew why or how they were started. Was it because no one wanted to come forward? Kyle knew very little about Dan and maybe a few suspected that the fires were started by him or his cohorts. Since he was never seen around again, the town just settled into an unsolved mystery.

Dan Masters had a cunning criminal mind and was used to getting what he wanted. He came up with another way to make a deal near Julian if he could wait this out. He served time for other earlier crimes including tax evasion, attempt with a deadly weapon, and unproven murder. Bench warrants awaited him in a few states for fraudulent activity, but he needn't go back there. He became greedier and felt justified using force to get his way no matter what the cost. When he read Tess's column, he panicked realizing some of the readers might come forward and reveal him. A sent text proved to be the lure he needed to end her curiosity. His pride kicked in when she agreed to meet him. Tess risked her life, but she may have been smarter than Dan realized. As he hiked toward the old road, he became livid because she was missing and he had no clue where, or worse yet, who she was talking to.

Jess drove up and Dan quickly stepped in.

"Oh, man. You look bad! What are we going to do about your injuries? You can't go to the hospital like that," Jess remarked.

"No, I'll be fine. Get me to your place and I'll clean it up. I can't let anyone see me looking this banged up. Tess is out there somewhere. I think we need to talk to that kid, Travis. He's a dirty little sneak, just like me."

"He burned his grandpa's barn. You got your revenge. What else is there to do?" Jess asked.

"Tess has a lot of dirt on the fires. She's been talking to everyone up here. I may have her camera and notes, but we need to get rid of her before she talks."

"You don't even know where she is."

"I'm going to find her."

"Dan, I don't want to go back to jail. Can we just forget about her, maybe move on?"

They both realized things were too precarious for their plans.

"You helped me do the job. Why are you getting cold feet now? If we get found out, it could mean prison for the both of us. You better keep your mouth shut or you'll be next."

"I heard you."

Jess knew who was involved in setting the fires. Some were paid to keep quiet. Jess was now having second thoughts about doing Dan's dirty work. More and more innocent people were paying the price.

Dan was unaware that Tess found herself in a safe place miles away. A few days had passed while friends and family were expecting her to call any day. No one had a clue where she was.

Chapter 6

The Meadow Knows Her Name

The air was especially warm on that day. The horses were kept inside, out of the summer heat. Many of the animals were kept in their stalls until sundown. Marion showed her how to prop the North barn door open with a bucket. At the right angle, it funneled the afternoon breeze through the building. Jeb figured it out years before.

Tess was getting used to waking up early with the sun. Each day, she went out to the stalls. The animals learned to like her. They would come out and beg for her attention. Tess felt like they were children greeting her as she brought them food. Even in the afternoon when she was not feeding, they would bleat or whinny at her. She loved to feel the horses after they were brushed. She would talk to them like Marion would.

She noticed sores appearing on her hands when she stopped wearing her gloves.

"How are those blisters doing? I'm not sure why you stopped wearing the gloves," Marion noted.

"They were getting in the way. I think they're too big."

"Just keep wearing them and they will adapt. Well, my goats just love you. I know when my Jeb was up early, he would call out, 'suey' to the pigs. They would come a runnin' when they heard him."

"That's a nice memory."

"Come on. Have some lemonade with me on the porch. It's breezy sitting right here."

Tess sat next to Marion as she poured an ice cold lemonade. Her glass began beading up instantly.

"Has Jeb been gone long?"

"He battled his sickness for about ten years. It was leukemia. He had good days and bad. I was happy he lasted that long. This farm meant everything to him. He passed away before the fires happened."

"What's the story about the fires?"

"Don't rightly know. It's a long way from here but the effects of it drifted over to our town. Many of the people there were my friends. To see them lose everything just cut me to the bone. Kyle's mother, Cheryl was my best friend. We went to high school together. I guess you could say, Kyle and I both lost someone we loved."

"Someone should do something to help."

"We did raise a little money to rebuild, but some homes are still sitting unrepaired." Marion had to take a breath. "Hey, this is no time to be mourning the past. We got good things right here and I'm so happy you are here with me."

"I like it here."

"Good."

The phone rang and Marion got up to answer it.

"Hello."

"Marion, it's Kyle. Is Ryan there?"

"Yes. I'll go get her."

"Ryan, it's for you. It's Kyle."

Tess got up and went inside where the phone was sitting.

"Kyle?"

"Hey, Ryan. Are you free later? I want to take you someplace."

"Well, I'm finished with my chores. What time are you thinking?"

"I'm done with my last patient by three."

"Do I need to bring anything?"

"No. I'll see you soon."

Tess walked back to sit with Marion. Her face was lit up.

"Now, that's a smile. What are you up to?" Marion asked.

"Kyle wants to take me somewhere. I don't know where we're going, but he said he'll be here after work. Is that okay?"

"Sure, it's okay. Kyle has a big heart. He grew up fast and became stronger when his parents died."

She became quiet and Marion put her glass down.

"What about you, are your parents still around?" Marion asked.

"They live far from here." Tess hoped it sounded convincing so Marion wouldn't suspect.

When Kyle came to get Tess, Marion was standing by the front door.

"Go have a good time," Marion waved her on.

"We shouldn't be too long."

"Those two are sure a pair. I wish I was young again," Marion said to herself.

She went back into the house to prepare hot rolls for dinner. Marion had a feeling in her heart that Kyle was smitten by Tess. She hoped both of them would find happiness like her and Jeb did. Tess had become more comfortable since she arrived. She was learning so much about herself and farm life. Marion couldn't help but think that maybe she needed Tess in her life too. It was nice to have young people around.

Kyle pulled out onto the road and drove for miles between open meadows splashed with colors of greens and browns intercepted by outcroppings and scrubby forests. On the other side, a golden wheat field waved, welcoming them home. When the road turned and meandered up through the hills, the scenery changed to taller trees and boulders. They passed a sepia toned barn that stood alone after surviving it's builders. She rolled her window down and smelled the air. It was clean and warm. With her arm out, she felt the wind wrap around her skin. Kyle could see she was happy. This was a world that agreed with her.

"What do you think?" he asked.

"I just love it! It's so beautiful. The land is so wide open and breathtaking."

"Now you know why I love it here."

They turned off of the paved road and found a winding dirt sideroad leading to an unfinished house. It was obviously being remodeled. Tess took a look at the house and the burnt trees around the property. Her memory jolted.

He stepped out and bragged, "This is the place!"

"It was affected by the fire," she sadly said.

"Yes. It was my parents' home. I'm slowly renovating it. I'm doing the work myself, so it's taking a while."

"You said you live here."

"I do. Behind the house, there's a small camper trailer. I just sleep in there, but most of the time I stop by Marion's for a meal."

"It looks like it is almost finished."

"On the outside. Let's go inside. I'll show you what I've done so far."

Tess couldn't believe the beauty around the place. She could imagine being there at night watching the stars blanket the night sky. Tess commented on the burnt trees.

"They will survive, won't they?" she asked.

"They'll heal soon. Look, they are already getting new leaves. I think the fire does something to the earth to help them recover stronger than ever," Kyle educated.

He unscrewed a sheet of plywood covering the back door and invited her to step in first. It was much cooler inside and their eyes took a moment to adjust from the bright sunlight outside. It was surprisingly clean and smelled like sawdust. The floor was new plywood, the wall studs were exposed and awaiting insulation. Pipes and white wires were woven between walls and the ceiling framing. An area in the living room had tools set up and ready to use.

"I made sure to get the roof covered first so the inside wouldn't get further damage. Later, I will put the metal roofing on. I would rather do the work myself. It's kind of an obsession with me seeing it was my family home. I feel the need to be the one to restore it since it was theirs."

She looked at the passion in his face, "I can see why it's so special. I like it."

"It's such a big house, probably too big for only one person. But I just can't seem to let it go."

"I love all these windows facing the meadow. I could just stand here and breathe it in. When I hear the wind, it calls my name."

"That was beautiful. Are you a poet?"

"I wish I could write. Everything about this place makes me feel happy and full of life."

There was a silence between them and then she asked, "When did you first know you wanted to be a vet?"

"A long time ago."

"When?"

"When I was in first grade, we had a pet rabbit in our classroom, Oreo. He was white with black spots and I loved him. We don't know what happened after a few days. When we walked into the classroom, he had died. It was hard going to school and not seeing him again. I thought about animal care ever since. My dad sold some of our land to pay for my schooling. I stayed in the city and started college. Have you ever been to San Diego State University?"

"I don't think so."

"That was over five years ago and I came back eighteen months later and started right in."

"Did you like the city?" She was hoping he would say something else she would recognize.

"No. I missed all my friends, especially Marion and Jeb. Dad built an extra room in the back of the house for me, like a studio apartment. I guess he wanted me to stay on."

"Where were you when the fire started?"

"I was supposed to be home. I had to stay overnight at Mrs. Garvey's house while her cow gave birth. I slept in the barn that night after the calf arrived. Edna came in and told me our home was on fire. By the time I got here, the firemen said they couldn't get to my parents' in time."

"That must have been devastating."

"I have to make my peace with it. It's strange, but I never did get to say goodbye. My heart still breaks when I think of them."

"I think what you do for the community helps you recover."

"I hope so."

His eyes were glassy as he gazed through the picture window at the horizon. She felt the urge to move toward him and offer comfort.

"What can I do to help?" she asked.

"Just being here is good for me. You are the first person I have had up here. I just couldn't let anyone in, until today."

She put her hand on his arm, "I'll be here for you."

Kyle looked at his home differently that day. He felt the fire burning inside to finish the home he loved so much. There was something about Tess and the way she walked the house that made him feel like he was in a good place. Emotionally, he was experiencing something new. He never took a good look at anyone's heart. Even though Tess's memory was gone, her soul was still apparent. Lately, he was having trouble getting her off his mind when she wasn't with him. He thought about giving her an invite to spend time with him.

"Hey, do you want to go with us to the Apple Picking Jamboree? Julian does it every year and it's a big event. I think you would love it."

"It sounds fun."

"Marion is coming with us."

"Thank you for inviting me."

"I want you to come."

The weekend of the Jamboree, they parked in a dry field next to the roped-off area. The three of them entered and found where the pies and cider were sold and the festivities were taking place. Each year, a pair of horses pulled a wagon full of straw. Tess looked at it draw up and Kyle watched her.

"What is that?" she asked.

"Haven't you ever been on a hayride?"

"No. I see people getting on."

"That's what they do. Would you like to take a ride with me?"

"Is it safe?"

"Of course, let's go."

Kyle held her hand and helped her up. The touch of her hand made him feel good. He sat next to her and they were jolted as the wagon started abruptly. She leaned into him, bumping his arm.

"Oh, I'm sorry. I need something to hold on to."

"You can hold my arm if you like. I used to do the hayride when I was a kid. My mom had a booth for quilts she sold. Some of her friends were quilters and they always shared tips on how to create patterns."

"It seems like your parents were a big part of the community."

Kyle heard the clip-clop of the horses pulling the wagon as he spoke.

"Yeah, they were. I was angry when I first lost them. I felt like I was slowly dying from the loss and pain. Marion came to my rescue after I isolated myself and refused to live. She nurtured me back to life. What's your story?"

"My story? What do you want to know?"

68

"Do you have parents?"

"I do. But I don't know my parents."

"Oh, I'm sorry. Is there a reason for that?"

"I have no reason; I just don't know them. Marion is the closest thing I have to a mother."

"You know she and Jeb couldn't have children. She wanted to turn her farm into a petting zoo to bring the kids over. But her heart was just too broken after Jeb died. I guess you could say, we needed each other."

"How has that helped you find some happiness?"

"I know it sounds silly, but I needed to be loved. Marion knew my mother. They were best friends in school and were really close. When Mom died, Marion naturally filled in."

"I know you don't know me that well, but I want to thank you for telling me a little about your back story. I wish I could express myself better than I do."

"I want to know more about you. You seem so held back. Maybe, someday you will help me know you better."

"It's not as easy for me to talk about myself. I will fill you in when the time is right."

"I hope so."

She held onto Kyle as he moved his hand around hers. There was something special happening and it was wonderful. Tess was new to love and wasn't sure what to expect. Sitting there next to him, she tried to remember things about herself to express openly and honestly. Nothing came to mind and it frustrated her. She did realize that she needed to keep the accident and the man in the car a secret until it was safe to share, even with Kyle.

Marion was sitting in the shade of a booth comparing the pies for sale. After the ride, Kyle and Tess joined her.

"Hey, you two! How was the ride?"

"It was fun. I little bumpy, but nice."

"Kyle, you should show Ryan where she could pick some fresh apples. Go take a walk through the orchard and show her how to do it."

"Would you like to?"

"I'm up for it."

Walking through the orchard, they watched dozens of folks from the community filling small buckets and bushels full. It was like a parade to watch so many of the young and old enjoying themselves.

"I got us a bucket. Are you ready to try?" Kyle nudged.

"I would like to pick from this tree."

"The ones on the ground are the sweetest for making jam and applesauce." Tess noticed some of the fallen apples and the bees that loved the sweetness.

"How do you know so much about how to prepare apples?"

"Well, don't forget, I grew up here. It's what we do. Many people from all over love to come here for the apple pie, but there is so much more. It's a beautiful place to live."

"Do you think you could teach me how to make apple jam or applesauce?"

"I'll even throw in a lesson on how to bake an apple pie!"

Tess laughed, "I'd like that."

Kyle helped her climb the ladder to reach the apples she favored. He climbed up the other side and smiled at her.

"You see this? This apple is almost ready. It still has a lot of green color and when you pull on it gently, like this, it stays on the tree. The ripest apples have the most sugar and come off easily."

"Like this one?" she pointed.

"Try it," he suggested.

"Oh! That was easy. Let me try another one." At that she dropped the apple in her basket.

"Remember, a ripe apple will bruise easily if it gets bumped. Try this." He laid another one softly in her basket.

Despite what she had been through, Tess was enjoying her company with Kyle. He made her day and the smile never left her face. After they finished, Tess looked around at all the people crowding the area. She wanted to go someplace less busy.

"Can you take me someplace where there are not so many people? I'm feeling overwhelmed."

"Sure. Let's sit over here."

They managed to find a shady spot under a tree near a small pond near a paddling of ducks.

"Is this better?" he asked.

"Yes. Thank you."

"Are you having a good time?"

"I am. Sometimes a lot of noise makes me nervous. I am glad to be here, promise. I just need a break."

"I can take you home if you're not feeling well."

"Oh, no. I'll be fine."

"Does that have anything to do with your head injury?"

"It could be the heat or I'm just tired. A glass of cool lemonade would help."

"Let me get you some."

As Kyle stood up to get her drink, Tess felt a wave of fear surround her about the accident. She didn't understand why her mind was tricking her. One thought would appear and then another without understanding why. She did not want Kyle to see it and she didn't want him asking a lot of questions.

"Here you go. I asked for extra ice to keep you cool."

"Thank you. It's perfect. Kyle, you are very kind and I am so glad to have a friend like you. I know we got off on a rocky start. I'm sorry for calling you a cowboy," she chuckled.

"No, it's okay. I kind of like it. I've always wanted to be one, so it was appropriately called."

"Please don't be too concerned about me and my brain. I assure you, I'm very normal."

"Well, I worry about you and I want to care for you."

Tess looked up at him smiling.

"I appreciate that."

"I'm a vet, as you are well aware, but if you feel like you want to talk to me about anything, even your health, let me know. I want to be there."

"I will."

It was a memory Tess would not forget. Her day with Kyle meant everything to her. It was another step in building trust with Kyle. In her heart, she was hoping that trust would grow into something more.

Chapter 7

The Search

Margo had been trying to reach Tess for a few days. It wasn't like her to stay out of touch unless she planned for it. Each time she called; Tess's phone turned off, either out of range or no charge. It felt too far off-center for Tess and it gave Margo an odd, suspicious vibe. She needed to report her worry to Digby.

"Hey, Digby."

"Hi, Margo. Have you heard from Tess?" Digby interrupted.

"No, sir." Her face revealed her fright.

He put his laptop down. "What's wrong?"

"I tried so many times. I called her, sent texts, checked emails, nothing. Digs, I don't know where Tess is."

"What do you mean? She always checks in with you. Did she inform you where she was going?"

"No. She mentioned how she wanted to go to Julian, but she changed her mind after she talked to you. She wrote that lifestyle piece for you instead."

"I was afraid of this. I told her she might get to interview the locals later, but I didn't think she would go without telling me first."

"Tess is a good reporter, Digby. Don't fire her because of this. Remember, she could have worked for any major network with her skill and experience. She chose to be here."

"I would never fire her." He stood up and began to pace. "Before we go into a panic, we should think of where else she would have gone to. Have you talked to her parents yet?"

"Not yet. I came here first."

"Ok, after we talk to them, we can put out an internet bulletin in Julian to see if anyone has seen her. I have some friends up there that might help."

"Let's get at it right away. Don't wait, Digby!"

"Let's be calm about this. First things first. I need to call her folks, just in case."

"I'm scared, Digby."

"Yeah, me too." He could hear the dial tone as he patiently waited for an answer.

Margo stepped outside his office hoping that if she tried one more call, Tess would answer. It wasn't normal. Why did that case have such a hold on her? Why was she so insistent on finding out undisclosed information about the fires? It would be like her to charge into the unknown to help the unfortunate in Julian. She would protect her friends and family from worry by not alerting them about her plans. It would never cross her mind that she might not return.

Digby finally connected with Dean. He imagined if he was a father, he would want to know the whereabouts of his daughter and Tess was like a daughter to him.

"Hello, Digby. What can I do for you?"

"Dean, I want to talk to you about a concern I have. Have you heard from Tess lately?"

"Not really. Well, several days ago she texted her mother. She gets so busy and we get used to her not calling much. She is always so focused on her job. Why do you ask?"

"Margo hasn't heard from her in over a week. Her phone is turned off and we have not been able to make contact."

"Do you have any idea where she might be?"

"She was covering a story about the Julian fires and wrote a fine column. She said how much she wanted to go up there and interview some of the victims and their families. I think she might have gone there."

"Should we call the police? I know that arsonists can be very bad people. She would never get too involved with them, would she?"

"No. I don't think she wanted to take it that far. Why she hasn't called us or informed her own parents, is a concern."

"I should talk to Sarah about this. Her mother and I should call the police and have them investigate to see if she has been spotted there."

"Good idea. I don't think the police go out that far. Dean, I know a couple of guys up there at the Sheriff's substation. I can send Tess's picture and info to them. I will also put an announcement in the paper that she is missing with your permission."

"Go ahead, do whatever you can. I'll call the Sheriff to get some officers to check around Julian. Thank you, Digby."

"We'll find her. I promise you."

Dean slowly put the phone down as Sarah walked into the room. He was visibly shaken.

"Dean, who was that?"

"It was Digby. Have you gotten any calls from Tess recently?"

"No, why? Where is she? What did Digby want?" Sarah fearfully asked.

"She's been missing for a while. They think she went to Julian."

"I'm going up there! I need to go find my girl."

"Sarah, going there won't help. You couldn't do any more than the law. I'm going to call them and get someone to investigate if they've seen her or her Jeep."

"I knew something like this would happen."

"If you think the worst, you'll go crazy, dear. If we let the authorities do their job, they will find her."

Dean made the call and talked to an available Deputy. He provided the latest about his daughter and what she was working on. Since it had been over twenty-four hours since they heard from her, it was approved to open up a case. An email arrived from the paper with Tess's ID, description, and profile to start with. Within the hour, officers were compiling a search file.

"Hello, Henry. Thank you for returning my call." Deputy Mattson was a friend of Henry Calhoun's.

"It sounded urgent."

"There is a reporter missing named Tess Charlton. She may have gone to Julian to cover the fires from last year."

"Kind of a brave, or stupid thing to do since we have all been trying to solve this case for a while. How long has she been missing?"

"I'm not sure. Maybe a few days. Get your team looking for anything related. I'm emailing you her profile right now."

"We'll get it done. Keep in touch."

Deputy Mattson contacted her parents to let them know they were working on it. It was a frightening time for Tess's parents. They surmised from news stories that those who lit the fires were nobody to mess with. They appeared sly and cunning, knowing how to hide from the law. Henry Calhoun sensed the fear in the area and some citizens were not ready to share. He was going to figure out why Tess was so adamant about coming. Little did they know, she was over fifty miles away from their substation. Some of the people remembered a reporter recently asking questions, but vaguely recalled a face or name.

Henry had informed his team. Over by the counter, Dale thought about the Bronco found up at Caspian's forest. A longshot in his mind might actually not be so long.

"Hey, Henry. I'm not sure if this will help, but Jim and I found that wrecked SUV in the forest north of here. We looked around and found no one. The driver side had some blood, possibly from the driver's injuries."

"Were there any other clues left behind? ID, registration, a wallet?"

"No. We ran the plates and it turns out the car was stolen from out of state. We towed the truck down to impound and started a DNA process. I haven't heard anything come back yet."

"I'm not sure if it has anything to do with Miss Charlton. Go over your report again and do a thorough perimeter check tomorrow around the site. You might find something more thrown out of the car. We could definitely use that DNA sample."

"You know, it rained the day before we found it. Pretty hard to find tracks or use the dogs after that."

Officers took Tess's photo to the local businesses. No one confirmed her existence, not even the cafe. With no sign of Tess, clues seemed to dry up. Henry was getting frustrated. It was killing him that there was no answer until his phone rang.

"Hello."

"Henry, it's Dale. We found Tess's car. It was parked near the café. The doors were still locked. The manager said it has been parked there for a while. It's being towed back to the station now where we can search it."

"Was there a purse in the car?"

"Didn't see one. Just the regular stuff in the glove compartment."

"That's not odd. I grew up with four sisters and none of them left without their purse."

"Anything else?"

"No. Thanks, Dale."

The DNA profile finally arrived. Three individuals showed up as two men and a woman. One of the men was from Texas with a RAP sheet a foot long. The other two could not be confirmed as a match. If Tess was in that vehicle with this dangerous man, she would want to escape.

Henry knew he had a job to do. He didn't want to assume Tess was kidnapped, but it looked too much like a crime and they had some tough work to do. Having a heart for the father missing his only daughter was getting to him. He was going to find Tess, dead or alive. He then remembered the young reporter who lost his life recently writing the same story and the search took on new meaning, almost an obsession. No matter what it might take, Tess must be found.

Chapter 8

Change Came Easy

It had been weeks since Travis drove Tess to Marion's farm. She had become a big part of the land, learning to cultivate, witnessing the birth of new animals and loving every minute. Previously, Tess had not taken the time to learn how to cook. When she lived in her apartment back in the city, she often ate take-out or an occasional bowl of cereal. Coffee was her drink of choice alongside the hustle and busyness of city life. Tess became a changed woman since becoming a farmhand. She even favored iced tea over coffee. Helping Marion in the kitchen, she learned to prepare meals and cleaning the house became natural to her. A hot bath before bed helped ease her tired muscles after working from sunup to sundown. She no longer needed Marion to wake her. When the animals stirred outside just before the sun rose, she was on her feet and ready to work. She enjoyed being around the animals like her own family. She would talk to them and brush them as they bonded with her. They knew her too. As soon as they saw her, they would quickly get up and go to meet her. They often expected her to bring carrots or grain. She loved how it felt when they ate out of her hand. When it came time to harvest from the garden, Kyle and Marion would help her learn how to choose which ones would go to the table and which go to the animals. Kyle would take a box of surplus vegetables to his vet's office and share with those who needed it. Life was good for Tess. She enjoyed every minute she was on that farm. She felt secure because, as far as she knew, she was hiding herself quite well.

One of the does was going to deliver soon. She overheard that she was beginning to nest, a prequel to kidding. Tess wanted to monitor her comfort in case she went into labor. When she couldn't sleep in the middle of the night, she got up, slid her boots on, and went out to the barn. Marion heard the noise and went to check. When she discovered that Tess wasn't in bed, she put on her robe and boots. Opening the barn doors, she saw Tess laying in the hay next to the goats, sleeping. Marion began to see what Tess was all about, a loving and caring young woman who had a good heart. She cared about the doe so much, she wanted to be her support.

"Don't that beat all," Marion said under her breath.

Tess woke up. "Oh, hello, Marion. I must have fallen asleep."

"I think Annabelle is happy you stayed with her. If she is going to have twins, she may need your help."

"I worry about her. Kyle said she is ready to deliver any day."

Marion knelt down next to them and began petting Annabelle.

"How is it going with you two?"

"Who?"

"You and Kyle."

"We're just friends. You know, he took me to his house a few days ago. It made me sad. He still misses his parents. Everything about that place was beautiful."

"He's never taken anyone there. Do you see how special you are? You obviously mean something to him, that he would share something so personal with you."

"I can't remember the last time any man was chivalrous. It touched me when he talked about how much he loved growing up in that house."

"Many of his friends have asked to help him on it, but he always turns them down. He preferred to work on it at his own pace. He thinks if he goes too fast, it will feel like he's letting his family go too easily. He doesn't want them to be erased out of his memory."

"He will always treasure them."

"Memories are very precious things to have. Without them, we lose all of the reasons why we laugh and love."

Tess began to realize that losing her memory meant she lost thoughts of friends, family, and especially her mother and father. There were many times that Tess tried to remember, but that just created more frustration. Often a word or a thought would enter her mind, but there was little to tie it to. Nothing was coming through and she missed what she didn't know about herself. She had to accept who she was. It wasn't that she didn't like this new life, she just had so many questions about her past.

"Is it okay if I stay here permanently, with you ?" Tess asked.

"You can stay as long as you want. We all love your company," Marion winked.

As Tess laid back down next to Annabelle, she thought again about Kyle and where it was going. As far as she knew, she never had a relationship or knew love. She couldn't deny that she was feeling something for him. It was wonderful. At the time, she wanted to be a good friend and wait to learn more about her feelings.

As Tess awoke a few hours later, she had strange thoughts. Flashbacks of faces that she couldn't recognize appearing and disappearing. She could hear a name being called by a woman's voice. It bothered her trying to make sense of it. She stood up and walked over to the horse trough and splashed some water on her face. Her hair got wet and she felt flushed. She began panicking about those intrusive thoughts. Feeding the animals their morning rations might help shake the feeling. When she felt better, she walked into the house.

"Good morning, farm girl. Did you take a bath in the trough?" Marion asked with a chuckle in her voice.

"Oh, no. I just needed to wake up. It felt good."

"How's Annabelle?"

"Still pregnant and very uncomfortable, a little restless."

"Any day now. Breakfast won't be ready for another ten minutes."

She took a bath and came downstairs. Through the screen door, she saw Kyle walking into the house.

"Right on time. Good morning," Tess greeted.

"Good morning to you."

"Did you get a new shirt? I like it."

"Yeah. My other ones all have animal stains on them."

Kyle washed up at the kitchen sink. The skillet was smelling good. Marion poured hot water over a tea bag for Tess.

"Kyle, Ryan slept in the barn with Annabelle."

"Really?"

"I think the doe appreciated that she was there. They sure love her."

Kyle looked directly at Tess, "I can see why."

Tess smiled but looked embarrassed. After breakfast, she washed the dishes while Kyle dried. He couldn't help but watch how she knew her way around the house. She was wearing a white cotton dress and her feet were bare. Wet laundry that Marion washed earlier needed drying and Tess went out and hung them before Marion could. Kyle stepped outside to get his medical bag from the truck. He wanted to check on Annabelle and treat some of the other animals for ear mites. He always made the animals feel like they were getting loved. On his way back, he glimpsed Tess hanging clothes. He stopped walking. With the sunlight behind her, Tess was glowing. The rays showed her silhouette through her light dress. Kyle was smitten by the curves of her body and was mesmerized by the beauty of a mysterious stranger. He was still puzzled as to why she never talked about herself. He didn't want that to get in the way of how he was feeling. He was spending a lot of time with Tess and he loved the gentle side of her. Kyle forgot why he was holding his medical bag.

He heard Marion from the living room, "Why don't you two go take a walk? The weather is perfect right now."

"Sounds like a good idea. How about it, Ryan? Are you up for it?"

"I could use a walk. I need to stretch my muscles out after sleeping on an animal mattress."

Kyle and Tess walked past the stables toward the trail and picked up a short, dry twig and nervously bent it. He looked at her strolling beside him. She always seemed to be amazed at her surroundings.

"I wish I knew more about you, Ryan. You're an amazing person. Is there a reason you don't like to talk about yourself?"

They walked several more feet before she swept her hair behind her shoulder and closed her eyes for a second.

"I guess I like listening to other people talk about themselves. I like learning. You are always interesting, but there's really nothing very fascinating about me."

He stopped walking and turned toward her.

"Are you kidding? You moved out here on your own with nothing. You learned how to care for these animals. Marion loves you and...I love you. You've really adapted." he complimented.

Surprised, she shifted her weight. "What? What did you say?" Tess quizzed.

"I said, 'I love you.'"

His eyes were dazzling in the sunlight. She finally turned her gaze away from them and looked at the ground.

"Kyle there's something about me that I need to tell you."

"What, that you were a horse wrangler in your past life?" he chuckled.

"No, I came to life when I found this place. I left behind a world that I might never get back." Tess lifted her head and admitted, "Being here makes me a better person. You and Marion made it happen. I have changed who I am."

"How does it feel to have changed that part of you?"

"Beautiful, it feels beautiful!" She reached for his hand and affirmed, "Because...I love you too."

Kyle bent his face closer to look at her, exploring the features of her face. The breeze was blowing her hair around. He put a palm on each side of her cheeks

and gathered the whisps back from her face and his
hands came to rest alongside her neck. Their eyes
fixed on each other and they moved closer and kissed
softly. Neither had any idea how long. It could have
been a few seconds or it could have been five
minutes. Time stood still. Without memory of what a
kiss felt like, Tess adapted quickly. She trusted
herself and reacted naturally to him. In the open
fields, two had fallen in love.

Both were learning who they were. Tess's primary
focus had been getting her memory back. That
changed after falling in love. She didn't want to go
back. She wrapped her arms around his waist and
watched the sun continue in the southeast.

"Let's tell Marion," Kyle suggested.

"I think she already knows. She's up on the porch."

Kyle could see her sitting up there, probably smiling.
They knew she wanted happiness for the two of
them. Both Kyle and Tess knew they were needed on
her farm.

He wrapped his arms around her and lifted her. Kyle
then twirled her around once. He felt he would do
anything for Tess. His confidence gave him an idea to
save the community and the town that was still
holding on to fear and sadness. He wanted to do it
with Tess by his side.

The next day was a mowing day. Marion's neighbor
used his tractor to cut the hay in the south field and
bale it later the next week. Tess learned from Marion
that it was important for the hay to dry out to
prevent combustion. Barns were known to catch on
fire when a farmer baled it too early. The next week,
Tess and Kyle loaded heavy bales into the truck to
stack inside the barn's loft. It was fun at first but
within a few hours Tess's muscles began to feel the
burn. Grass poked her arms through her flannel

shirt. It was hot and Kyle thought it would be a good time to rest. Marion brought cold water.

"You are a pretty hard worker."

"Thanks. I am enjoying it," she smiled.

"You can drive the truck this time."

"What? No, I don't think so."

"You've never driven a car before?" he asked perplexed.

"I never drove a truck."

"The field is empty. It is a perfect place to learn to drive."

"Oh, I don't know."

"Come on. Let's give it a try."

She watched Kyle drive many times. She wasn't sure if this was a good idea. She turned the key. The truck came to life and she stepped on the brake. She pushed on the gas pedal next and it leaped forward. She turned the wheel to the left, missing the chicken coop. Bumping up and down around the field they toured until she slammed on the brake near the fence. Suddenly, Tess had thoughts about being thrown in a crash. Her mind could feel her body coming forward and hitting her head on the dashboard. She gasped for a moment, not realizing Kyle was next to her.

"Are you okay? What is it?" Kyle was concerned.

"I just got a little stunned." She was breathing heavily and staring at the steering wheel.

"I didn't mean to frighten you. I just wanted you to learn."

"No, you did nothing wrong. It just shook me up."

Tess was thinking about her memory loss and what being in that accident must have done to her. Whatever life she used to have was not as important as her new home, yet her mind was trying to get her back to who she was. She never expected her amnesia to take over and recovery could change everything for her and Kyle.

Chapter 9

The Paper Trail

Sarah was sitting on the bed in Tess's childhood bedroom holding her teddy bear. Dean had been looking for her throughout the house. When he found her, it was obvious that she had been crying.

"Honey, why are you in here?"

"I was thinking about our little girl. Remember when she was five? She wanted to be a reporter her whole life. When she went to Afghanistan, I feared the worst. Now, my fear has come true," she wept as she leaned into her husband.

"Sarah, don't do that to yourself. They found Tess's car. She has to be safe nearby. She is a smart girl and wherever she is, she'll come through fine."

Just then the phone rang and Dean answered it.

"Hello."

"Dean, it's Detective Henry Calhoun."

"What news do you have for us?"

"We found nothing unusual in Tess's car. The man in the wreckage has no evidence of being in her car. Looks like she rode with him up there. Her DNA was found in the passenger seat. They are combing the area to see if they can find anything more."

"Do you think she is alive?"

"I would like to think so. She didn't die in the accident so she may have got out before he did. The blood from the DNA of the driver belongs to a man named Mitchell Clemens."

"Never heard of him. Who is Mitchell Clemens? Why would Tess know him?"

"He has a record. We're not sure why Tess was in the car with him. He could have been someone who knew something about the fires or Robbie. Since they survived the crash, they are both out there somewhere."

"My daughter's injuries could be serious."

"If she was able to walk away, she might be okay. All we can do is keep trying to find her and figure out why this man was with her."

"Thanks for all of your help."

"No problem, Dean. You and your wife keep having hope. We got this."

Dean hung up and stayed by his wife's side providing comfort. They had to believe that Tess was alive and safe. It was hard to not think of her experiencing trauma or injuries. Where could she be?

The Sheriff took some volunteers to rake and search for the day. They needed to uncover anything that would give them an idea why there was no ID in or around the car. Dale was determined to locate anything suspicious. They had been working around the eastern side of the forest for hours.

"Sir, I think we found something!" one of the men shouted out below.

"What is it?" Dale asked.

"Looks like a bag. I'm putting my gloves on. I'll bring it up."

After finding nothing else, the volunteer delivered it and Dale examined it closely.

"There appears to be nothing inside the backpack. We can take it to Henry. Put it in an evidence bag and we will wrap it up." He shouted out, "Let's pack it in, crew! We've been here all day."

Dale walked into Henry's office and held up the empty khaki bag.

"They found it thirty yards from the crash against some leaves. Probably thrown there after the crash. Do you think it's hers?"

"We won't know until we get it tested. It doesn't look like it's been out there for more than a couple of weeks. Ah, it's killing me there is no ID. The guy who was with her knows something. He may have taken what was in the bag with him. A reporter would probably carry her notes in there. She wouldn't throw it. I'm not sure who got out first. It's baffling."

"We put out flyers everywhere and asked the townspeople. It's so weird no one remembers Tess in town. Even the server at the café where her car was parked said she doesn't remember."

"I think they might know more than they let on. Folks we asked are scared to come forward. They don't realize how it will help and not hinder them. We just have to keep asking around until we get someone willing. Someone knows something."

Henry ordered the bag to be examined and remembered a resident he knew most of his life. It was time to go visit John Samuels, a man whose house was partially burned. He hadn't been able to rebuild due to the lack of funds even after his insurance reimbursement.

"John, it's good to see you," Henry greeted.

"Well, well. What are you doing here?"

"We've been doing more investigating for that missing reporter."

"Why are you coming to me?"

"I wanted to know if you happened to have seen her recently."

He turned and walked to the back of his house where a small travel trailer was parked. Henry followed.

"John, you're my oldest friend. I know you hate the cameras and news people asking you all those questions. But it's just you and me now. Don't be afraid to talk to me. I want to help."

John nervously put his hands in his pockets and tilted his head, "Alright, alright. There was a young woman here. She was asking too many questions about my house and the other places burned."

"Can you tell me what she looked like."

"Dark long hair, she dressed casually, she had an ID tag around her neck she handed me. She was driving a Jeep."

"She didn't look injured?"

"No, she was well put together. I asked her to leave my property. She wouldn't stop prying me with questions. So, I made it look like this wasn't my place so she would stop interrogating. I didn't want it to get back to Masters that I said anything."

"Masters? Who is that?"

"Oh, some guy who wanted to take over the world last year. He wanted some of us to sell him our pieces of land for below value and he'd give us a huge return after he sold shares to investors. When the town council asked him to leave Julian, he never came back."

"Dan Masters. He wanted land and was kicked out by the council. Are you sure he's gone, John? What if he's holed up nearby and still around?

"Well, I haven't heard anything from him. So far, I think he disappeared."

"So you say," Henry said in disbelief.

"What do you mean?"

"I think he might have something to do with that wrecked car north of here. Although, the blood in the car was from another man, or another name." He looked toward the sky thinking.

"That reporter woman was only here once."

"Her family is very worried about her. The man in the car could be dangerous."

"He's a forceful guy. We called him, Dan the con man. He pressured me and few others, making his veiled threats. Maybe the man in the car wasn't him."

"I'm not so sure about that. He may have taken on an alias. The car was stolen. John, I know it's been hard coming forward with what you know. You're information is safe with me."

"I don't want any more harm to come to me or my property. Who knows when I will ever get that house repaired. I hope you find the young lady."

"I hope we do too. Thanks, John."

Henry stopped by to question another land owner, but the gate was locked. It looked like no one had driven the road for months. When he had more time, he planned to question other victims in the week. Many of them were still afraid and in due time, they might feel more comfortable revealing things. He was perplexed about this Dan Masters. He called the council to see if they knew anything not yet uncovered but could only leave a voicemail. He would get one of the officers to call them individually when they got back in the office.

Travis was getting ready to leave the feed store and head home. At seventeen, he still lived with his parents. On his way, his phone buzzed. It was Jess.

"Trav, are you someplace where we can talk?"

"Why are you calling me? Once I did your deal, I told Dan I wanted nothing more to do with any of you."

"What do you know about that woman reporter that was up here recently?"

"A reporter? I don't know anything about that."

"Are you lying to me? She was in a car accident and now, she's nowhere to be found."

"I really don't know any reporter. What do you want?"

"I just hope you haven't been giving anyone any information about me or Dan. You are just as guilty and it could be a bad thing for you if you talk to anyone, including that nosy reporter."

"I haven't been talking to anyone. I wish I never got involved with you two. Now, stop calling me!"

"In your case, money talks and you listened. Five thousand dollars is a lot of money to a kid like you. Your family is fooled by who you really are. It would be a shame if they knew about what you did."

"I don't want the money anymore. I still have it."

"We had a deal. It's best you keep quiet about what you know. You set fire to your own grandfather's barn. How could you do that to your family?"

Travis never spent the money. He kept it safe. Returning it could mean danger for himself and his family. He wanted to give it back, but Dan refused it.

Jess did his best to be intimidating. Travis was having serious regrets getting involved with the wrong side of the law.

"If anything gets out, we know who to blame and where to find you."

"You don't have to threaten me! I won't say anything."

Jess hung up. Travis was feeling afraid for the first time and thought of going to the authorities to confess what he knew. How could he do that without revealing his own guilt? Seeing that he was just as culpable, he had to keep quiet for the time being. He stopped to think about what was said about a reporter in town looking for clues. He had something stuck in his mind that he just couldn't remember. It was something he saw at the feed store that made him think about an accident. He couldn't put his finger on it.

Chapter 10

Where The Sunrise Ends

Tired after working all day under the sun's heat, Tess was falling asleep on the couch. Marion suggested she go to bed for the night, she deserved it. Tess fell asleep quickly but awoke later feeling agitated. Her mind wouldn't rest and thoughts came in and out that made no sense. She opened the window to feel the breeze touch her face. The room felt stuffy. She laid on her back and watched the sheer curtains lightly blowing and felt the night air cool her body. She was able to relax and fall asleep again. That night, she talked in her sleep as she watched haunting and mysterious images. She heard a name being called out.

"Tess, Tess come back to me," the voice cried.

She could see the faces of two people running to her, reaching out to touch her. She tried to respond, but they couldn't hear her. Again, she could hear the voice calling her.

"Tess, it's Mommy. Please come back. Tess, Tess."

Her body was sweating and anxiety swept through her body. She tried to scream. No sound came out. As the faces came closer, they became distorted and the sound of the voices were muffled. It scared Tess and her body twitched.

She fearfully shouted, "No! No! Help me!"

Marion came in to comfort Tess and found her trembling.

"Ryan, what is it?" Tess's hair was clinging to her sweaty forehead. "You had a bad dream. Let me get you some warm milk," Marion suggested.

"No. Stay with me, please." Tess was still shaking and pleading with Marion to not leave her.

Marion was more curious about Tess's past. She wanted answers about who this woman was, what happened to her, and why was she so terrified? It would have to wait until morning. Without adding to her anxiety, Marion wanted to support the girl she had grown fond of. She was worried about her and just knew there was a good explanation for Tess's anxiety. Marion knew she had to trust her and whatever the problem, she was prepared to honor that trust. As Tess fell asleep, Marion slept next to her and put her hand on her arm to assure her she would not leave. It was hard for her to sleep thinking about what she could say to help Tess.

The next morning, Marion was up at five, feeding the chickens and the dog. She put fresh water in Codger's bowl. Tess was still in bed.

Two hours later, Tess finally came downstairs. She didn't feel like herself and she had a headache.

"Good morning, Marion."

"Good Morning. I made some tea for you."

"Thank you. I'm sorry I slept late. I guess I'm not feeling well."

"You had a nightmare last night. Do you remember me coming into your room?" Marion was pouring hot water into her cup.

"No. What happened?"

"I spent the night with you. You begged me not to leave."

Tess realized she was having those reoccurring thoughts that gave her anxiety. It was more frequent and vivid and it disturbed her.

"Come sit with me," Marion encouraged.

"Okay. You look like you want to talk to me."

"Yes, dear. I do."

Tess was feeling nervous because she suspected she was on to her about what happened. Marion put her hand on to hers and squeezed gently.

"I have been giving this a lot of thought and I want you to trust me. Can you do that?"

"I think I can. I'm not sure why you are asking me that."

"When you came here, you didn't tell me or Kyle anything about yourself. You kept quiet and then these regular nightmares. You have times when you look confused and forget to do simple things, like close the gate. I have to take more time out of my day to check on the animals. I want you to talk to me about what is going on. You can trust old Marion. Tell me who you are."

Tess stopped to think about it. She felt it was probably time to come clean and tell Marion what she knew about her journey. She deserved the truth.

"I'm afraid to tell you."

"Let me say this, I've kept some juicy secrets. It's what happens when you live in a small town. Now what is it? Go slow if you need to."

Tess took a breath and tried to remember what she knew.

"I don't know who I am. I don't have any memory of my past life. I woke up in a car with a man who was unconscious. The car was badly wrecked and I escaped without knowing what happened or why I was there."

Tess began to cry silently. She brought her hand to her face. So many emotions began to release as she explained what she went through.

"Oh, my dear. So, your name is not Ryan?"

"No. It's just a name I picked up at the feed store. I am afraid of the man in that car because I don't know why I was with him. I felt this strong urge to escape and got away before he woke up. I got out through the broken window and my body hurt all over. I was glad to be alive. I came here to hide away until I got my memory back. I didn't mean any harm to you or Kyle." Tess continued to sob feeling regret for imposing.

"Marion, I never wanted to hurt you."

"I know. Dale came by the day you were dropped off telling me a car was found up at Caspian's forest. That's a long way from here. Was that the car you were in?"

"Probably. I'm not sure if that man was alive. I was afraid I may have been linked to a crime and he was dead because of me."

Marion slid her chair around to hold Tess. She wouldn't judge her. Instead, she praised her for being brave enough to trust. Marion didn't know Tess was a reporter. She just wasn't the type of person to care much about the news or the gossip in town.

"Dale said there was no one in the car when they found it."

"What? The car was empty? He was out cold when I escaped."

"The driver is still out there. You know nothing about him?"

"No. I mean, there must be a reason why I was in the car with him, but I have no explanation."

"Should we tell Kyle?"

"No, please don't tell him. I'll find the right time. Let's keep this between us for now. I need you to protect me until I can remember more about my life. I don't know my real name or anything about my parents. Will you help me?"

Marion put her hand on Tess's face and promised to tell no one. Tess wanted to go about her life as if she was always on the farm. Her experiences of drawing close to the animals, confirmed she would never go back to the life she once knew. Was it even possible for her to live how she used to? Would she remember her parents or continue reporting? At the time, it was easier not knowing who she was.

Her happiness came from Marion and her farm that put a smile into her heart. She didn't know much about love, but it was powerful. What she felt for Kyle was genuine and she could feel her heart aching for his arms. She was safe with him and she could only guess why. There was something special about the way he spoke to her and expressed his feelings about his losses.

Tess learned the role of a mother from Marion. She was nurturing, loving her and her animals. She loved when she was held, touched, and treated tenderly. That kind of comfort was what Tess needed to bring her back to reality. Tess felt like it was her real home.

Kyle was at his home making a list of the work that needed to be done. He realized he had been procrastinating. Was he afraid that finishing his home would mean that he let go of his parents? The thought crossed his mind. He had to change the layout of the home to avoid traumatic memories of where their bodies were found. He wanted to start from the foundation up even though some of the house was fine. It was his rash decision to tear most of it down and start again. He had plenty of money to finish but looking at his father's life insurance account made him emotional. It was unbelievable to think they were really gone. The day he brought Tess to the site made a difference. It spurred him on and impelled him to invite her to work on it with him. He sat outside of the house on a sawhorse looking at the land his father protected from those who wanted to take it away. It was his grandfather's property given to Kyle's father when he died. He could see himself as a boy running and hiding, playing in every corner of his then world. Looking at the meadow, the sun drifted downward and the sky took on ombre hues of pink and purple. The horizon came to be special to him. He never stopped to just look at it enough to appreciate it's beauty like Tess did. He just sat there and stared at the vast amount of grasses as far as the eye could see. He shed a tear as he dedicated it to his beloved mother and father. They would want him to move on and finish what he started. He decided to go to Marion's to talk to Tess. It felt good to just drive there without thinking about anything else. Tess was who he needed to run to.

"Well, look who's here," Marion announced.

"Who is it?" Tess asked.

"Kyle."

"Remember, don't say anything."

"I gave my word. Go to him. I think he's really here for you."

Kyle got out of the truck and walked up to the porch. He could hear horses whinny and chickens clucking. The windmill was making a chiming sound. Tess came out to meet him.

"Kyle, shouldn't you be at the clinic?"

"I asked another vet to cover me for a few days. I needed to take some time off to decompress."

Tess looked at him perplexed not knowing what that meant.

"Well, why are you here?"

"I've been thinking about it and I just had to see you. I've been looking at my land and realized how much I want to honor my parents and finish the house. That property has been in my family for years and I can't stop thinking about you standing there looking at that meadow. You brought that house to life again. Ryan, I want you to help me."

"Help you do what?"

"Rebuild my family home. Will you?"

"I don't know how to rebuild a house."

"I'll show you. I will teach you how to do whatever it takes to bring the place back. What do you say, you want to help?"

With Tess's memory affecting her life, she was nervous trying new things. Because of her deep affection for Kyle, she would not let her ailment keep her away from the man she adored.

She stepped forward looking up at him, "Yes, I'll help you."

He couldn't help but take her in his arms. It was impossible for them to take their eyes off each other.

"Thank you. I don't want anyone else but you. I just can't get it out of my mind. You standing there; like you and the meadow are one. It was beautiful and I want that to be part of the new memory for this place. My parents would have been happy to have known you."

Tess smiled. She couldn't help but wonder if she had parents she might see again. For now, this was her family and being any place else was not what she wished to focus on.

Chapter 11

Regrets

Travis had been thinking about the conversation he had with Jess. He was feeling the pressure to keep information about Dan to himself. He was young and desperately took any offer that was exciting, enticing, and hard to pass up. Everyone thought Travis was a good kid and he had been before meeting Dan. No one suspected that he would be coerced into helping a criminal get his way. The young boy had no idea how typical it was for Dan to get other people to do what he wanted. Farm life had not prepared him to stay free from a professional conman. Travis believed that if he could talk to Dan, and let him know what he was feeling, it might ease his conscience and reduce the threats. He was still trusted in the community, and it was easy to hide what he knew and did. But maybe, it was time to come clean. How could he without risking his life? The more he thought on it, the more afraid he became, thinking of what Dan might do to him. Worse yet, what he might do to his family. He had to think harder about what was needed to get out of it. Because he did not want to face them again, he was fearful to return the money. If he did give it back, that would not resolve the threat. It did not feel like a contract that could be broken.

With Travis's mind racing, he remembered the day's chore. He had to meet his friend Davey and purchase a calf for his father's farm. Near Julian, there was a small farm with a few healthy animals for sale.

"Travis, did you eat some breakfast?" his mother asked."

"Yeah. I gotta go meet Davey to pick up the calf."

"Make sure you get a heifer and this time make a better offer."

"Okay."

Just as he was leaving the house, he got a text from Dan.

"I need to talk to you."

Travis's nerves intensified and chose not to answer. He wasn't sure what he would say anyhow. What would Dan want to speak to him about? Would he repeat what Jess said? He dropped his phone in his pocket and drove his truck to pick up his friend.

Pulling onto a long graveled driveway, Travis slowly approached Davey's place to avoid dust.

"Hey, thanks for coming along, man."

"No problem. I was trying to find an excuse to get out of raking the stalls."

"I haven't been to Julian in a while."

"Are we only picking up one calf?"

"Yes."

After they made their offer and paid for the heifer, they decided to get a bite to eat.

"Hey, you okay?"

"Why would you ask that?" Travis asked.

"You look nervous."

"I just have some stuff on my mind."

"You wanna talk about it?"

"No. I'll be fine."

They parked across from the café that served sandwiches and other lunch specials. As the boys walked up to the entrance, Travis saw a picture of a missing woman. He stared at it until he realized it was the woman he saw in the feed store.

"What is it?" Davey asked.

"I know this woman. I met her a while ago. She was acting weird when she came into the store."

"Do you know where she is?"

Travis hesitated. "Uh, no. She left after she used the restroom." He felt uneasy with his lie.

Travis didn't want anyone to know he had seen the woman under the hoodie. He knew he gave her a ride to Marion's. If he revealed where she was, it might not be good for him and the secret he was keeping about Dan.

"Do you think you should go to the Sheriff and tell them you saw her?"

"No! No. It's not my problem. Besides, she could be anywhere."

As Davey went into the café, Travis took the flyer and put it in his pocket, making sure no one saw him.

While the boys were eating, Travis couldn't stop thinking about Tess. His phone vibrated another text from Dan.

"Why aren't you answering? Call me right now!"

"I need to answer a text. I'll be right back."

Travis decided to call Dan back.

"Hey, what do you want?" Travis asked annoyed.

"Next time answer when I text you. Where are you?"

"I'm in Julian. I'm going home soon. I'm not alone. I'm with Davey."

"Jess said they are looking for that missing reporter. You wouldn't happen to know anything about her, would you?"

"No. But I know there are flyers all over town. Why would I have anything to do with her?"

"Something tells me you know something about her. I hope I'm wrong."

"You are wrong. Why are you asking me?"

"Let's just say she knows something about our little operation. And if you get found out, it could mean jail for you!"

"For me? You are just as guilty. I should have never gotten involved with you or Jess."

"Having regrets? Well, it's too late for that. If I find out that you know where this woman is, you are going to be very sorry you ever met me."

"I don't want to do any more jobs for you, no matter how much you pay."

"Just think what it will do to your family if you are found out, Travis. Think about it."

Dan hung up the phone. The intimidation was powerful. Travis went back into the restaurant to tell Davey he needed to go home.

"What's wrong? Who were you talking to?" Davey inquired.

Travis replied despondently, "Never mind. I need to get the calf home. We have a long way back. Could you drive?"

He flipped the keys in his direction.

"Sure. Whatever it is, we can talk about it, okay?"

"No, it's fine. I just want to go home."

Travis didn't say a word on the way back. He had a lot to think about. For a grown man to play on a young teenager without a record and con him into committing arson, was weighing on him. He wanted to go to the police with what he knew, but then kept asking himself, 'what would that mean for me?' What would his parents think of him and what he did? As he slumped in the passenger seat, he recalled the day he met Dan. Travis just got the job working for the feed store.

"Hi, sir. Can I help you?"

"Hello, young man. Do you know a Nathan James?"

"Sure, but I can't tell you where he lives."

"How would you like to make some money, help me out?"

"Oh, I don't know. What do you want me to do?"

Dan showed Travis a large amount of money in his satchel.

"Looks good, doesn't it? Think of what a kid like you could do with this kind of money."

"What do I have to do?"

"Maybe we could talk outside."

"I can't stay outside too long. My boss will catch me."

"Well, you already have the makings of a criminal."

"I think I better stay inside."

"Come on, kid. This could all be yours if you do just a little something for me."

Travis wanted the money. After being instructed on how to set a fire without getting caught, he was paid in cash. When told to torch more homes, Travis refused. Just burning down the barn was enough to bother his conscience. Dan forcefully pressured him to do as he was told or else. After that, Travis no longer wanted contact with either of them. The guilt swept over him knowing he was an accomplice to their crimes. It was a dilemma that bothered him and there was no one to help. Would it help if he went to Marion's and talked with Tess? Somehow that felt like an easy way to figure it out. The next day, Travis drove over without calling.

"Well, Travis. I'm surprised to see you. What are you doing here?" Marion asked.

"Oh, I thought I'd see if Kyle was here." His eyes kept darting around to see if he could locate Tess.

"You're a long way from home. You should have called him at his clinic. What's on your mind?"

"Uh, we got a new heifer calf and I wanted to talk to him about it. Oh, how is your new hired hand?"

"Ryan? She's doing well. Would you like to say, hello?"

"Okay."

Tess stepped out on the front porch.

"Hello, Miss. Nice to see you again."

"Hi. I'm sorry I'm bad with names."

"Travis."

"I got some biscuits out of the oven and some coffee made. Come on in, Travis. Stay a while," Marion motioned.

Travis remembered that the flyer revealed the missing woman's name as Tess Charlton. He tried not to stare at her. He didn't want to make them suspicious by asking too many questions. He then realized Marion called her Ryan.

"How do you like it here at Marion's so far?" he quizzed.

"I love it here."

"You look much better than when I met you."

"How are your parents, Travis," Marion abruptly asked.

"They're good. My dad started a goat farm. The cows don't mind."

"Goats love this part of the county."

He turned his head away from Marion and asked as casually as possible, "So, Ryan. Do your parents live close by?"

"No. They live in another city."

"Which city?"

"Travis, why don't you go give Kyle a call to see if he is coming by today," Marion interrupted.

Tess got up from the table and put the dishes in the sink without giving Travis an answer. She was feeling uneasy with his questions. Why was he asking her where her parents lived? She was thankful that Marion distracted him with other conversation.

"You know, I should take a ride over to your folks place and check out those heifers. I bet your dad got some beauties out there in the pasture."

"The new calf makes a great addition to the herd."

"Did you still need to talk to Kyle?"

"No. I should be on my way. Your hired hand doesn't talk much. Is she alright?"

"Ryan? Oh, she's just a little quiet. I'm trying to get her to talk more. She's a good worker and she's kind to the animals."

"Where'd she come from?"

"Makes no difference. I don't care about that. She is the best thing I've ever done for this farm. Why the sudden curiosity from you?"

"That's it, just curious. Thank you for your hospitality. I better go now."

Marion watched Travis through the screen as he got into his truck. She hadn't learned about the flyers posted in town about Tess. But it was very odd that Travis made the trip to her home to talk. Marion found Tess in her room.

"How are you doing?"

"Why was he asking me all those questions?"

"I don't know. He is still young and I don't think he knows about you. Just a youngster being curious, I guess."

"There are so many times I almost told Kyle about my memory and the accident. I still don't remember what happened that day. What if I did something bad or caused someone to be killed?"

"Darlin,' you did nothing bad." Marion went over to hold her. "This will all work out soon. I'm sure your loss of memory is only for a short while. When you are ready to tell Kyle, you'll know. Until then, your secret is safe with me."

"Thank you for being here for me. I no longer feel lost. It's all because of you and Kyle."

Travis drove the long way by his grandfather's barn on the way home. Parking out front, he just stood there staring at the damage he caused. That barn had been in his family for years and it gave him a lot to think about. He had to do something, even if it meant being punished for committing a crime. He didn't know where Dan lived or where Jess was. He reasoned that if he turned himself in, they might never get caught for what they did and the law would blame him. He wondered if Tess had anything to do with Dan. Travis remembered overhearing his father talk about a car wrecked and abandoned in Caspian's forest, and a week later about the missing woman. He also recalled Tess covering her head and face with her hoody, maybe covering a head injury in the feed store. Was she innocent or was she part of Dan's conspiracy? Before he could tell anyone about what he knew, he needed to get answers from the one person who may know, Tess.

Chapter 12

You Have Changed My Life

Kyle finished installing the new roof on his house. He wanted it done before Tess arrived to help with other improvements. Most of the electrical and plumbing were completed by two local contractors who traded veterinarian services for working on his home. His plans for the day consisted of installing drywall and cleaning up dust accumulated during the project. Kyle changed his clothes and drove down to see Tess, hoping to convince her to spend the day with him. He was impelled to have her share in the work. Each day he realized the rebuild wasn't something he wanted to do alone. Tess didn't realize it, but she had helped him make his decision to complete his beloved parents' home. His picture of her standing in the sunlight, made finishing the job more of a delight than a chore. The first night after bringing her up there, he couldn't sleep. His thoughts persisted about her. It was her love of Marion, her farm, and care for her animals. She was always talking to them and showed concerned for their well-being. Many nights she spent the night in the barn watching over the mothers and babies. She was tender and patient without aggression. He could see her true heart. His thoughts kept coming back to the fact that he was in love, something he never had with any girl he had dated before. Working on the house together, meant a part of Tess would always be there. When he would roam the halls or enter the bedrooms, he would think of her and how she contributed to the ambiance of his family home. She would leave her mark in every room.

Tess waited for Kyle. She had no idea what she would do and she did not care. She was making new and beautiful memories and wanted it that way.

Tess could not realize that her memory might affect her relationships with others around her. She had bouts of thoughts coming in and out, some scaring her, causing fear. Since Marion knew what she was going through, Tess's anxiety attacks could be managed with the help of her dear friend. Memories struck unexpectedly and caused questions that slowly revealed her true identity. Somehow, being with Kyle never caused her fear. She loved the life she was living with him and she didn't want that to change. She would lay awake some nights wondering, 'what if Kyle knew about me?' She wondered how he would handle it. Would he understand or abandon her because of her secret? There were many questions going through her mind, yet she never questioned his affection for her. That was clear and she was falling deeply with the thought of spending her life with him and not worrying about the past. But that was not reality. Tess's mind may heal and she would regain some of her memory. She would have to learn how to deal with that. For now, Kyle was special, a feeling that made it easy to live in the present.

"I have a surprise for you," Kyle said with a smile.

"What is it?"

"I'll show you when we get to the house."

Riding in the truck, Kyle reached over and held onto Tess's hand. Tess loved his touch. Because she wasn't herself, it was all new and she felt like learning how to love felt good. Driving over the rise up to the house, Tess noticed how beautiful everything looked.

"You got the roof finished!"

"Yes. I thought you could help me with landscaping and painting outside. I need your input on colors."

"I'd love to help. I don't think I've ever painted before. What if I'm not good at it?"

"Who cares? We'll just say it was a mark on your workmanship. I don't mind if you make mistakes."

Tess came inside and went right to work, noticing the floors needed sweeping and trash taken out. Kyle put up the rest of the drywall. After cleaning the inside, Tess went outside to start painting the trim. Kyle came out to guide her, trusting she would make the house look lovely. Kyle picked out a white trim and showed Tess some swatches of colors for the body of the house.

"What do you think?" he asked.

"I love this one," she pointed to a color sample.

"Oh, you like blue. That is called Sky's Reflection. I like it. I'll put in the order today."

After the heat became intense, they decided to take a break and have some lunch. Tess looked at Kyle's trailer in the back. She had never been inside. She didn't know what it was like to live in a small space for such a long time.

"Would you like to sit inside the trailer? It might be cooler than sitting outside."

"Okay."

When Tess came in, she noticed it was very clean. On one part of the wall near the kitchen hung pictures of animals and thank you cards from Kyle's patients. On one side of the wall was a picture of Cheryl and Nathan during happy times. The bed was made and the dishes were washed and put away on floating shelves near the window overlooking the meadow. It was small but perfect size for the dedicated vet. Kyle turned on the air conditioner.

"I made us some sandwiches and Marion gave me some of her iced tea which she says is your favorite."

"She knows me so well. Thank you. I love all the pictures on your wall. Do you still keep in contact with any of them?"

"Some have moved away; others are still regular patients. Sadly, some of these pets are no longer with us."

"Oh, I'm sorry to hear that. I have never lost a pet before."

"Do you prefer cats or dogs or any other pet?"

"The closest thing I have to a pet are the animals at Marion's. I have never seen an animal die."

"Unfortunately, it's part of the job when you are a vet. It never feels good to put down someone's loved one or companion."

"Put down?" Tess asked.

"Euthanize, having to end their life so they no longer suffer."

"I've never known much about that."

"No one likes to talk about it, even me. It's not something I like to do when giving bad news. Most of the time we get them back to health."

"Marion's animals are very healthy."

"I know Annabelle is set to deliver soon. I want you to be there when the twins come."

"I'd love that. I have slept in the barn with her many times. She lays next to me, keeping me warm."

"She was a rescue and I knew the best place for her was Marion's. It's been a good fit ever since. Now she's going to be a mama." Kyle took a sip of his tea and looked at Tess, wanting to pose a question.

"Ryan, do you ever think about leaving Marion's to go back to where you came from?"

"No. I hope Marion will keep me on as long as she wants. I have no place to go back to."

"What happened that made you decide to come here?"

"It's complicated."

"Whatever it is, I'll understand."

"I just can't tell you much about what brought me here. I don't think I can talk about it."

"You don't trust me?"

"Of course I trust you. I need more time to expose that part of my heart. Please respect my feelings about it. I promise you; I will tell you more about myself when I'm ready."

"I guess I have to respect that. I feel like there is so much bottled up inside you, Ryan. I need to know about you."

"You will. You know how I feel about you, right? Live in the moment with what we have today and all the days we're together. I am true in my heart and I know I will always love you."

"I could live on that for years. I love you too."

Kyle could feel that the love he felt for Tess was everlasting. Her devotion and love made the moment possible for him. Finishing the house was all about her. He tried not to assume she was hiding anything from him. He wanted to trust her and time would have to pass before she would say more about herself.

They worked into the night so they could watch the stars together. Sitting on the back deck, Kyle brought a blanket for Tess and a warm cup of tea from the trailer. She could hear crickets chirping along the fence grasses and feel the cool night air lightly touching her face.

"Warm enough?" he asked.

"Yes. I love it out here. The sky looks so beautiful. You must have some relaxing nights sitting here alone."

"Sometimes. I reflect on how much I miss my parents. My mom loved looking at the stars. She knew all of the constellations. It was one of the reasons why Dad put a big picture window in their bedroom. Like you, it was her favorite spot."

"People in the big city will never know what this is like unless they live it. I have that privilege and there is nothing more I need than to be here with you."

"I can't wait to finish the house. It's going to feel so weird moving in. I often think, what if I can't live here? It might be too hard."

"No, it won't be. You have me. We can get through it together. Nothing is impossible for us. I will carry you through all the pain you fear."

"What is it about you? What makes you this beautiful person who isn't afraid to carry someone else across the current? You're beautiful, Ryan. Thank you for being my biggest support."

Tess smiled at him and kissed his soft lips. After opening a bottle of beer, they talked into the morning and fell asleep in the chairs on the deck. When daylight came, Tess noticed Kyle still asleep. She went inside the trailer to heat some water and noticed Kyle's backpack and cell phone sitting on the counter. Tess stared at the backpack. Noises swept through her mind.

"Don't forget your backpack," she heard a voice say.

"Where are you taking me?" she heard again.

She became afraid and saw the man in the car. His face was clear but no name came to her. She shook her head and reached for a glass to fill with water. The images became more vivid and she could see herself being tousled in the car and then blacking out. She

117

blinked and then gasped, dropping the glass onto the floor. Kyle heard the glass shatter and ran over to find her staring.

"Ryan, are you okay?" he noticed the glass at her feet.

"Yes, I'm fine. I'm sorry. It must have slipped out of my hand."

"That's okay. Are you sure you're fine? Let me take you home."

"No, I just need some air. I can clean it up."

"No, let me do it."

Kyle picked up the broken glass off the floor and walked it to the trash can. He could see Tess standing near the oak tree staring at the meadow. She was crying. He wasn't sure if he should go to her or let her alone for a while. He was puzzled as to why she had times when her moods would change. Whatever it was she was going through, Kyle was feeling the need to help. In his practice, it was his job to be supportive. This was no different. He loved Tess and nothing would stand in the way of caring for her. He gave her a few minutes and then approached her.

"Ryan, are you feeling better?"

"Yes. I think I'm just tired. We did go to sleep late."

"I wanted to make us some breakfast. I'll start it and after we eat, we can go to Marion's."

Just as Kyle was making breakfast, his phone rang.

"Marion? What is it?" He could hear her voice as if she was crying.

"It's Annabelle. She's in labor and I think you should get here right away. The kids aren't coming out!"

"How long has she been in labor?"

"All night. I stayed with her and now I'm worried."

"We're on our way."

"What is it?" Tess asked.

"Annabelle's in labor. We need to leave right away."

He sped up to make good time.

"Kyle, we should slow down a little."

"I know. I don't want to lose Annabelle."

They made it to Marion's. Kyle honked the horn to let her know they were here.

"Hurry! She's in the barn laying on her side. Please don't let her die," Marion cried.

"Don't worry. We'll get those kids out."

Kyle had Tess grab his medical bag and follow him to the barn. He could see the doe was in pain. Her water broke and she was bleeding. He could see hoofs partially out as she pushed to deliver. She stopped having contractions so Kyle reached in and gently pulled on the kid.

"Ryan, put your hand on the mama and comfort her as I pull."

Tess watched as Kyle did his best to save them. She could hear the doe bleating as she tried to push.

"Come on, mama, push!" he urged.

"What's happening?" Marion asked.

"Nothing yet." Kyle could feel his heartbeat as he struggled to relieve the doe.

"I have to pull harder. You can do it. Come on!" Kyle put his hand further into the birth canal.

Tess was nervous but trusted Kyle would know what to do for the doe. Marion looked on, holding faith Annabelle would be alright.

"Okay, this is it. Almost coming home, baby!"

Out came the newborn. The doe gave birth to a buckling. He noticed he was having a hard time breathing.

"Ryan, put this towel around him and rub him here, like this. Get him to breathe."

A few minutes later Kyle delivered the other one, a doling. Annabelle was laying down as the doling came to nurse. Tess was doing all she could to get the buckling to breathe. Kyle tried to get him to come to life and then he petted the kid on the nose and whispered, "So, so sorry little one."

Kyle looked up at Marion and Tess and announced, "We lost him. He was probably in distress all night."

"You did what you could," Marion said as she touched Kyle on the shoulder.

"I'm sorry, Marion." Tess hugged her.

They laid the buckling on a sheet to bury him in and turned their attention to the mother and newborn.

"We should weigh the doling. She looks like a healthy weight."

"I'll get the scale," said Marion.

Tess stared at the buckling that had died. Both her and Kyle were still covered in amniotic fluid. Kyle was never comfortable losing an animal during birth. He could see it having an impact on Tess.

"Kyle, can I hold the buckling?" Tess asked with tears on her face.

"Are you sure?"

"Yes. I want to hold him."

Kyle wrapped him up and handed him to Tess. She held him gently observing what could have been new life on the farm. She wept and Kyle came to sit next to her as they comforted each other. This was something Tess had never experienced. She was a tenderhearted person by nature before her accident and her true persona came out stronger in the moment. Marion hung the scale to see the doling get weighed.

"She's seven pounds, eight ounces. Healthy looking too. Let's get her back with her mother. Marion, what would you like to do with the buckling?"

"We can bury him by the shed over there," she pointed.

"Whenever you're ready to let go, we can give him a proper burial, Ryan."

"I just want to say goodbye."

"Take all the time you need." Kyle could feel her pain as she held the dear one.

Marion went to pet Annabelle. She was so happy she was alive and at least one kid was saved.

"Kyle, I should have called you last night, but she was pushing and I have delivered kids before. I hope this wasn't my fault."

"No, Marion. It wasn't your fault. Annabelle will have another chance, kidding again in the Spring."

Marion went to get the coffee on. Tess was still very sad about losing a creature she had come to love and felt comfort holding the new addition to their family.

"What made it happen?" she questioned.

"It could be a lot of things. A blood clot in the placenta, not enough oxygen, who knows? I'm happy we saved one. They could've both died."

"The loss is hard to take."

"We all eventually move on. I'm sure Annabelle is grateful we helped her through it."

Kyle checked the doe one more time and took the deceased away for burial. Tess continued to hold the doling. She knew this was where she belonged. She had witnessed something beautiful, realizing how precious life was. She thought about how grateful she was to be alive after her own near-death experience. Tess realized she was slowly getting pieces of her memory back and didn't know how much longer she would be in that state. What would she do if her memory came back all at once? She repeated her gratitude; she was glad to be there, not thinking about her future.

Chapter 13

The Reveal

It had been over a month since Travis discovered Tess was the missing reporter. His family could see he was distant and isolating himself. Before he returned home from work, his parents were discussing what they should do with his grandfather's barn. Should they rebuild it or lease the land to neighbors? It never crossed their mind to sell it, although Dan tried many times to take the land for himself. Travis's mother, Doris, was concerned that her son was involved with the wrong crowd. While putting away his laundry, she discovered something in Travis's drawer.

"Tom, could you please come up to Travis's bedroom?" she hollered from upstairs.

"What is it, Doris?"

She pointed to the money in the drawer.

"Where did he get that kind of cash?"

"We need to get some answers. Where is he?"

Tom tried to keep his composure without getting angry.

"He's at work. I'm terrified he may be in trouble."

"We'll talk to him when he gets home."

Tom concluded, "No. I need to settle this."

Tom took the money out of the drawer and put it in a safe place. His concerns were based on what he noticed about his son. Since the townspeople were going through so much, they didn't need one more problem to sort out. Tom remembered Dan Masters and the threats he made to take their family's land they've had for generations.

Travis was home schooled and earned trust from the owner of the feed store to work part time hours. His parents wanted him to be responsible and help pay his way. They opened a savings account for him and monitored where his money was going. Finding that amount of cash made them leery and it didn't look good for Travis.

He walked up to the screen door and dropped his shoes on the front porch. As he walked inside, he saw his father sitting in his recliner. His mother was upstairs.

"Hey, Dad. What's for dinner? I didn't eat lunch. Where's Mom?"

"Travis, sit down, right here."

"What is it? You look upset."

"Son, your mother and I care about you. When my dad died, that barn was all I had left of his memory. I lost him and I don't want to lose you."

"You won't lose me. Why are you talking this way?"

Tom reached behind his chair and showed Travis the money.

"Son, what is this about?"

"Why are you going through my things?" Travis recoiled.

"Your mother found it. She wasn't going through your drawers. What's going on, Trav?"

"What do you mean?"

"Oh, stop with all the questions! You are involved with something. Now, we made an agreement that if you kept up your grades, you could continue to work at the feed store. You've done a good job so far and we've trusted you. But this has us wondering what you're up to. Are you selling drugs for someone?"

"No, I'm not selling drugs!" Travis was upset and nervous. Before he met Dan, he was honest with his parents and it felt like he was being forced to tell them about it.

"Be straight with me. Where did you get this money?"

He turned his head toward the front door, "I can't tell you."

"Why? Why can't you tell me?" Tom got up from his chair and ran his hand through his hair frustrated.

"I'm trying to work it out on my own. I wanted to give the money back, but they refused."

"They? Who are these people? Travis, this isn't looking good for you. You could bring harm to yourself and your family if you are doing something stupid."

"I know. I've got a plan. I'll work it out."

"Well, since you won't be honest about your dealings, you are grounded. I'm keeping this until we can return it to the right owner. Something tells me this is dirty money."

"Dad, I'm sorry."

"If you were sorry, you would trust me. I can help you with whatever this is that has changed you."

"If I'm grounded, can I still drive the truck for work?"

"You can go to work, but no friends and I'm giving you extra work around here. I'm very disappointed in you."

Travis felt even lower about himself. He wanted to reveal the truth to his father, but he was more afraid of Dan and what he might do to his family. Being young, he didn't know how to handle serious issues. He already knew too much about Tess and everything weighed heavily on his mind.

Travis left work early. He knew his parents wouldn't allow him to make any stops or visit his friends so leaving early was important to him. He could hold back no longer. He was going to talk to Tess again. He brought the missing person flyer with him. He had to save himself as well as Tess. Marion happened to be visiting a sick friend for the afternoon and Tess was alone. Travis didn't know how this was going to affect her, but since his parents found the money, it was time he told her. Tess came onto the porch and heard his truck turn off.

"Travis, what are you doing here?"

"I got off work early. I need to talk to you."

"What's on your mind?"

"I came here to tell you that I know about you."

"What do you mean, you know about me?"

"Your name is not Ryan, is it?"

"How do you know that?"

"Because of this." He pulled out the flyer and showed her the picture of a missing woman named Tess Charlton."

"This is you. Your name is Tess Charlton. It's obvious this is a picture of you."

"Where did you get that?" Tess was shocked to see her face on the paper.

"They're all over town in Julian. They're looking for you, Tess. Your family, everybody that knows you."

"There isn't anything I can do about it. I don't know what to do."

"Go home. Think of your family, they're worried about you."

"I can't go home! I don't even know where home is." Tess was terrified and couldn't think clearly. She was trying not to panic.

"Who else knows about you?"

"Marion knows." She had to sit down at the porch. Travis followed her.

"Does she know your name is Tess Charlton?"

"No, I didn't even know that."

"I heard about the SUV wrecked in Caspian's forest. You came into the feed store with a head injury. Remember? Were you in the car?"

Tess stammered. "I, I was. There was a man next to me and I don't know who he was."

"You were in the car with Dan Masters."

"How do you know that? Who is that?"

"Because I recognized his silver Bronco."

"How do you know him?"

"I met him over a year ago. My dad was struggling financially to keep the farm going and it sounded good to get some extra money for him."

"What did you have to do for the money?" Tess was afraid of his answer.

127

"It doesn't matter. The fact is, I shouldn't have got involved with him. He's a very dangerous man, Tess. You shouldn't have been in the car with him!"

"I don't know why I was in the car with him!"

"You are a reporter. You were probably trying to get information about the fires. That's my guess."

"I don't know."

"What do you mean, you don't know?! You were in the car with Dan Masters! Why are you acting like you don't know anything?"

"Because I don't! I don't remember what happened before the accident. I've lost almost all of my memory! I have been having anxiety and nightmares, it's just plaguing me. I don't know how I got here or anything about my past. I keep having these flashes of images in my head about this man. He keeps telling me that he wants to help me."

"Dan Masters doesn't want to help anybody. He only cares about himself."

"Why do you know so much about him? If he's such a bad man, why are you involved?"

"Like I said, I shouldn't have been. But now it looks like both of us are involved with him."

"Now you're telling me I'm linked to a crime?"

"Well, no, I'm not saying that. I'm telling you that you were with him and I'm pretty sure he was going to hurt you."

"What should I do?"

"Just go home. Let them know you're okay."

"I told you, I can't."

"Does Kyle know?"

"No. Don't tell him. I'm not ready to tell him about what happened."

"I'll keep your secret safe. I know I'm young and it doesn't look like it right now, but I am usually a good person. I did something stupid and made a big mistake. I want to help you. I want to help both of us. Dan could be coming back for you."

"Why don't we go to the police? Why don't we tell them what you know? Why would he come after me? Travis, I'm scared."

"I can't go to the police."

"Are you linked to something that's bad?" she asked frightened.

"I have to fix this on my own. Tess, you are going to need protection. The people who work for Dan are very treacherous. You will be caught in the crossfire if you get too close to them."

"I don't want to go home. Bringing me to Marion's farm was the best thing for me. Thanks for that. I don't want Marion to get hurt."

"I understand."

"Please don't say anything."

"Eventually they are going to find out about you. If the press gets a hold of this, they are going to find a way to bring you back home."

"I don't know what it will do to Kyle if he finds out who I really am."

"You came here to Marion's not only to hide out, but because you care about people. And Dan tricked you. Look, for the both of us, I will keep it safe. I gotta go. If I'm late, my parents are going to freak."

"Thank you, Travis."

"I want you to trust me. I know that is hard for you, but you have to trust me. I know more about Dan than you realize. Can you trust me?"

"Yes."

"Okay. I gotta go."

Tess receded into the house astonished over what she learned. It was coming back to her. She remembered the name Tess heard in her thoughts. There was still so much she didn't know about her life, but what Travis told her made sense. She didn't want to believe it, but when she saw her face on the flyer, she was shocked. What would happen if it got out and she was taken back to her home town? Her world would change and she would miss what she fell in love with. She had to believe that Travis would maintain their pact.

Travis made it home on time. Before he arrived, Tom got a call that Travis left work early.

"Travis! Where were you?"

"I was at work."

"Davey said you left early."

"I stopped by Marion's. It's true. You can ask Ryan."

"Who's Ryan?"

"Marion's hired hand."

"You were not supposed to go anyplace but work. Are you trying to stay in trouble?"

"No. I want you to trust me. I went there for a few minutes to just talk."

Tom was in disbelief.

"Fine! Don't let it happen again. Go clean the stalls and do your homework."

"Yes, sir."

It felt right, but he wasn't fully sure he did the right thing telling Tess who she really was. He was going to do the right thing by telling his parents of his involvement sometime soon. Before that, Travis would have to gather the courage to tell the Sheriff about Dan Masters.

Chapter 14

Robbie

As a child, Robbie loved writing short stories about clues requiring research. His favorite book character was Encyclopedia Brown. He knew it was fictitious, but he still aspired to become as aware of hints and cues around him.

Robert Charles Carnes finally became a respectable and well-liked reporter. Like his mentor Tess, he was always fascinated with mystery and intrigue of complicated cases. He considered joining the ranks of professional detectives, but his stronger passion was to report it. Robbie and Tess studied journalism at the same university a decade apart. When he interned at the paper, it was fitting that Tess mentor him on some of the tougher investigations. He was developing mental acuity· and experience to get inside information while avoiding trouble.

During his weekends, Robbie liked taking his dirt bike out to the desert and cutting loose. A sleeping bag, a box of granola bars, and a few bottles of water were enough for him. He checked the fluids and topped off the gas before he was able to take his ride. That clear morning awakened his senses. He breathed in the freshness that was so different from his city and strapped on his helmet. Off the gravel road and into the dirt, his bike was alive and responding perfectly. Down a swale and topping over a rise, he chanced upon several younger riders creating their own dust devils. After they stopped, they talked about where they were from and some of the best trails for their next adventure. Travis and Robbie became friends and planned to bike around the back trails of Julian. Especially fascinating, were the old gold mines with their intriguing history. Their age difference mattered little. The two hit it off and built trust in each other. Travis had a few ATV's stored in his parent's shed and he invited him to ride along with two other friends. After slipping between some huge granite boulders, Robbie noticed a pile of ashes where a barn once stood. Another mile over revealed a blackened building.

"What's the story on that?" he asked Travis.

"There's a lot you don't know about this place."

"Who burnt down these buildings?"

"I can't tell you."

"Why? C'mon, Travis. You know something."

"You have to promise you won't tell anyone."

"You got my word on that. What happened?"

"There was a rift between Nathan James and Dan Masters. Dan begged me to tell him where Nathan lived."

"Why? What did he want?"

Travis trusted Robbie, but the information could ruin their friendship and put them in danger.

"I don't know what he wanted from Nathan. I know a few people in town said they didn't get along. After they had words, several homes were burnt and destroyed. Dan made me swear not to tell anyone."

"Trav, that is arson! You should have went to the police."

"I couldn't. Dan will ruin my family and blame me for all of the damaged homes."

"I will stand by you. We're friends. I'm not sure why you would involve yourself with this kind of guy."

"I know. I made a mistake. I wasn't thinking straight at the time and now I want out of it."

"You feel safe?"

"For now I do. But if he finds out you know, it won't be safe for you."

"Where is this Dan Masters? Who does this guy think he is?"

"He did some serious time and he had to hide his identity. I heard Jess call him another name once. He used the name Edward Clemens. Maybe he has aliases."

'Travis, I'm sorry you did this to yourself. Why are you afraid to get help?"

"No one can help me, Robbie! I'll go to jail if I say anything else. Promise me you will keep this to yourself. Please, swear you will not tell."

"You sound like this Dan. You need to go get some help."

"Look, I want to let the authorities know, but it's not time yet. I need to work out a plan."

"A plan? You are an accomplice to a crime! You might be tried as a minor, but you can get free from this man."

"I can't. Dan will make sure I am to blame for the fires and the people who died. Then he will come after my family."

"Sorry you are in so deep," he empathized.

Travis goosed it and caught up with the others. Robbie followed behind a few feet to avoid the heavier dust. He never thought that his good friend would be involved with someone who hurt innocent people. It wasn't sitting well with him.

As they continued riding the roads and hills, Robbie's fun had turned to serious curiosity. Who was this arsonist and what was he trying to settle? Why was a young boy like Travis, even a part of their plans? He must remember the name Edward Clemens and do some research when he got back to his computer. He was feeling guilty. Did he really promise not to say anything about it? Travis had become a close friend and he would do almost anything to help him get out of his mess.

Robbie was able to do a couple of background checks on Edward Clemens using his laptop. He had to be alone to do this in a desperate attempt to help his friend. What he saw shocked him. After evading the law for years, he was jailed twice and spent time in prison. Caught with weapons during altercations, he was dangerous, ruthless, and cunning. Travis appeared trapped in this tumultuous relationship with this man and his henchman. If Robbie could get enough information and find a way to save Travis, Dan Masters, aka Edward Clemens, could be put away for good. Afterwards he researched the fires and read interviews from two of the victims. Robbie had become fond of the town of Julian and its surrounding mountains. He knew he had enough passion to go after these men, but he was inexperienced. Did he have enough to outwit them? He learned to question everything aloud from those he worked around.

"Why would Travis do this? I have to help him," he said to himself.

Robbie was not thinking realistically about saving him. He contemplated ignoring his promise and informing someone who could help. After completing his research, he texted Travis. They agreed to meet at the feed store after it closed, where they would ride together in Travis's truck. Travis locked the store from the outside. As he turned, he saw a face that made him nervous. It was Jess lurking close by waiting for him. Travis wanted to quickly get away from him. He knew he would have demands and would intimidate him into doing something to ruin his life. Travis just stood there in fear, knowing he was trapped. All he could do was face him and hope it would be over soon.

"What are you doing here?" Travis asked. "I need to go home."

"You don't have permission to just do what you want to. You don't rule your own life anymore."

"I'm staying quiet, I did what Dan wanted. I told him I was done with both of you."

"You think you can run and get out of this? We had a deal and now you have nowhere to go."

"I'm not interested in what you have to offer. I'm going home." He began to walk to his truck.

Jess pushed back and refused to let him leave until he talked to him.

"You wouldn't want anything to happen to your family or for them to be exposed to what you did?'

"What is the reason why you are here? I told Dan I would give him back the money. I don't want to do this with you any longer. Let me go!"

A car pulled off the paved road into the parking lot. It was Robbie. He saw Travis talking to a man. Suddenly, Jess shoved Travis knocking him to the floor. After shutting off the engine, Robbie rushed out of the car to get between them.

"Travis, are you okay?" Robbie demanded.

Jess fired back in Robbie's face, "This is none of your business, so I would suggest you get back in your car and leave," Jess did his best to sound menacing.

"You may think you can bully anyone with that speech, but I don't fall for it. Travis, what is this guy doing here?"

"Robbie, I'm okay. Wait in the car and I'll be right with you."

"No. I know about guys like this." He looked at Jess and forcefully barked, "Leave him alone and go back to the dark hole you came from."

"I guess you didn't listen the first time. This has nothing to do with you. If you want it to be, I guarantee you won't see tomorrow," Jess threatened as he stepped into his face. Robbie backed up a step and looked at Travis. Jess turned to be sure he was straight with Travis.

"Think about what I said," Jess repeated.

At that moment, Jess opened the door to his vehicle and vanished.

Travis had his hands in his pockets and Robbie could see the tension in his face.

"Why did you do that? Are you trying to get us killed?"

"Do you hear yourself?! It's clear this guy is bad news. You need to get out of this now! The police will help you get out of your trapped situation. They can help you."

"I don't want to start any more trouble. I'm protecting my family."

"They can protect you!"

"No! I can't take that risk. Can we just go and forget about Jess?"

"Jess? I thought that was Dan."

"Dan never shows his face around here. Folks don't like him."

"I can see why. I want you to think it over. I don't want to betray your trust and go to the police before you do."

"You would never do that."

"If I have to save your life, I will. You're my best friend."

Robbie wanted to get Travis out of the funk he was in and go someplace to relax. He remembered the place that they loved to go to before the troubles happened. They spent a couple of hours before dusk sitting together around a small pond. Robbie was throwing rocks in the water trying to calm down. This was bothering him and he had to rescue his friend from the atrocity.

"How are you feeling?" Robbie asked.

"I'm alright."

"You have to do the right thing. Coming forth will save the lives of others as well. I'm very sure these guys will harm anyone and not care."

"I didn't like Jess threatening you."

"Those were probably just words."

"No, man. He's a snake. I know he's in the same trap as me and when Dan forces you, he means business."

Travis's grandfather used to go to this pond when he was younger, remembering how he always told a good fish story. They liked talking about what they wanted to do with their years together. Travis felt better talking to Robbie and realized that he was right. Robbie put his arm around Travis assuring him he wanted what was best for him. His friend was going to try to talk to the Sheriff about his connections with Jess and Dan.

"You're making the right choice. Trust them. They have your back. You'll be safe after you put these men away."

"Thanks, man. I'm glad I have friend like you," Travis said with a smile.

Robbie would stand by him and give everything if it meant saving his friend. Losing daylight, the pond took on a new appearance. It felt more relaxing talking about their future than what Travis was going through.

Robbie had a long drive ahead of him and wanted to go home before it got too late. It was already dusk and it would be dark soon.

They arrived back at the feed store where Robbie's vehicle was parked. As he unlocked his door, Robbie took one last look at Travis.

"Stay safe, man," Robbie advised.

"Yeah. I heard your words."

"I know you'll do the right thing."

Travis waited until he got into his car.

"Hey, let's celebrate once this is over. It will feel good to be free again."

"You got it!"

There was a car parked off to the side of the feed store with its lights off, possibly reading a text message.

Unknown to them, a Mercedes Benz with two men were waiting for Robbie and Travis behind the store.

"Is that him?" Dan asked.

"Yeah."

"You know what to do."

The man in the parked car finished his texting and drove off leaving Travis out front. As Travis put his truck in gear, he seen the Mercedes speed off from out back and head west. He put his foot back on the brake.

"What?!"

The first thing that came to his mind was that Robbie was in danger. He should follow and warn him. As he turned his head to turn out, he heard a slap on the hood of his truck. Jess walked by his truck door. Travis was startled.

"Get home and don't get any ideas!"

"I'm leaving. Don't involve Robbie in this. Don't hurt him."

"I'm through with you. Your friend already got himself into trouble."

Jess walked away. Travis quickly drove eastward until he found his phone and tried to call Robbie. There was no answer. He didn't realize he had a dead cell phone sitting on the passenger seat. Robbie was tired and was thinking about work the next day. He didn't want to drive home that late, but he had no choice.

On his way back to the city, a few minutes passed before he noticed headlights behind him. They were following far too close. He put his hand out and waved the car around. The car did not attempt to change lanes and continued to tailgate. Robbie couldn't help but check his rearview mirror constantly. It was getting closer to the back of his car. When Robbie sped up to evade the driver, he felt a bump from behind. For a moment, he swayed and fear swept through him; what if he lost control? His heart raced faster. The road was winding steeply downward and one bad move could mean his life. He felt gravel under the right wheels rattle his suspension. He pulled the wheel harder left. Panic set in and he began to drive faster.

The corners were sharper and Robbie knew he was risking his life driving that fast. Again, his car was hit from behind. The road had only two lanes and there were no side roads, no houses, and no place to turn around. The next curve was posted at thirty-five mph. Tires rubbed hard against the pavement and slid with a terrifying screeching sound. At that moment, the enraged driver landed a harder hit that sent Robbie's car out of control. It's back end rotated to the right and struck gravel sliding out of control. The speed threw his car over and off the embankment. It continued rolling and bouncing over boulders until it found a place to rest near the bottom of the canyon, upside down with Robbie inside.

The driver got out of his car looking down and eyeing the wreckage, hoping it would end in an explosion. It never did. Without remorse, he climbed back into his car and drove away.

The next day helicopters found the wrecked vehicle and pulled Robbie's lifeless body out. News got out that a young reporter was killed. Authorities were busily investigating whether this was an accident or murder. Little evidence came to light. There was nothing to give a clue as to why he was targeted. His cell phone was smashed beyond recognition. Tess got wind of what happened and she was devastated. She broke into tears collapsing to the floor of her bedroom. She was fond of Robbie and she didn't want to think about what this would do to his family. Digby made a trip to Tess's home. She opened the door.

"Hey, girl," Digby said sympathetically as Tess ran into his arms.

"Digby! Robbie's gone."

"I know. I loved him too." He put his arms around her.

"Why? Who would do such a thing?"

"The Sheriff will get the answers. Until then, we can't say it was or wasn't foul play."

"He wanted to get information about the Julian fires."

"What? Tess, I had no idea."

"I think someone wanted to stop him from finding any information about who was involved."

"Sometimes as reporters, we want to do more than help. Robbie was as passionate as you."

Digby held Tess close as she cried out her pain for her good friend. She missed him and his life demanded justice.

At his funeral, friends and family gathered to remember Robbie. Many from the local newspapers and news stations attended to pay their respects. Those who knew him, understood he made reporting his lifelong career. Sitting in front, were his parents and his siblings. The turnout was amazing. Not just a few observers, but over a hundred attended. Tess wrote a few words to speak in front of everyone.

"Robbie Carnes was a phenomenal reporter. His passion was an example of dedicated journalism and getting the facts. We went to the same university and because I was older than he was, he asked me to mentor him. I was so honored to help him bring out the best of who he was. He was already good at what he did. His desire to keep improving, made me smile. He was my friend and nothing will ever change that friendship even though he is gone from us. I am so happy to have known him and I wish we could have spent more years learning from each other. Now, as hard as this is to do, we must say goodbye to a friend, a brother, a son, and a gifted person. We love you, Robbie Carnes."

Tess made sure to hug the members of his family. As they tearfully left the gravesite, Robbie's mother, Diane, came to kneel by the open grave and stared at her son's casket in the ground. She was holding a handful of roses given to her. Digby watched Tess run over, put her arms around her and let her take her time releasing her pain. The sky grew gray and a blanket of sadness covered the cemetery.

Tess couldn't get the mystery out of her mind of the night Robbie died. From there, Tess did not realize how wanting to change history would alter her own life and everything she worked hard for. When Travis found out about Robbie's death. He was in over his head and was more fearful than ever. He sat in his room and mourned the loss of his friend. He blamed his stupidity and couldn't bring himself to go to his funeral.

Months later, with Tess's slate erased, she had no idea about Robbie or the townspeople, except for her real name. Sooner or later, she would be found out.

Chapter 15

Solving the Puzzle

Travis realized how much he had ruined his own life and felt hollow without Robbie. Even though this was a bad thing for Travis, he continued to have dealings with Jess and Dan. They had their hooks in him and their pressure was too much to let go. He was holding powerful secrets. He did not need to add another to his life. The initial trauma was getting easier to bear by the time Tess walked into the store where he worked. Time had passed by too quickly and his plan had not evolved.

At the substation, Henry got word from the Sheriff. Using the bloodhounds, they matched her scent from her car to the wrecked Bronco and tracked on one side of the wreckage's location for several feet. After that, they lost the trail. The rain shower had washed away any leads they hoped for.

"Do you think she's alive?" Sheriff Dale asked Henry.

"I don't know. They may have kidnapped her or she's hiding out."

They had no idea that Tess had lost her memory. So many things were going through Henry's mind about why some of the folks would not say much about her. They had to have seen her when she came to town.

It had been several months since Robbie died. No one came forward about him or Tess. Henry was keeping his eye on some of the people involved in the fires. He got a tip from someone who wanted to remain anonymous. Henry was glad to finally hear someone come forward. It was obvious the town was watching out for themselves and their families. The person of interest asked to meet Henry late after hours to avoid being found out or followed. He agreed.

"Are you prepared to tell me what you know?" Henry asked.

"Yes, and I need you to protect me. I've been wanting to tell Dale, but I wasn't sure if he would keep me safe."

"You did the right thing coming to me. Why did it take you so long to say something?"

"I was afraid. I heard something the night Robbie Carnes died."

"Were you there?" Henry could see the fear as he tried to unfold his story. "Hey, don't be afraid. I got you. I want to help. What else do you know?" Henry probed as he put his hand on his shoulder.

"I pulled over to answer a text in the feed store parking area and I overheard two men talking. My lights were off and I rolled down my window to hear their conversation."

"They didn't see you, did they?"

"No, They were around the back. I didn't want them to know I was there. I wasn't sure who it was. Their voices carried, so I got every word. They were talking to a boy named Travis. Then I heard them mention Robbie and that they needed to get rid of him, making it look like an accident. I had never heard of Robbie before that. Then I read about him in the paper a few days later. I guessed it was probably the same guy."

"Are you saying they killed Robbie?"

"I don't know for sure. I heard one say, I'll take care of it, and the other one said, good for nothing coward.

145

Then I left. I wanted to say something, but I just couldn't risk my life."

"I understand. Thank you for coming forth. I won't mention you. By the way, did you get a good look at the car?"

"It looked like a white sedan."

"Thanks. I need to talk to Travis."

"I think he's involved in some kind of mess. He's just a kid and I'm not sure he knows how to get out of what he is into. I hope this information can help him."

"I hope so. Oh, by the way, have you heard anything about this missing reporter that was here a few months ago?" Henry asked.

"No. I hope Travis isn't responsible for her missing."

"Thanks, again. Go home and if you hear anything else, call me."

Henry was disturbed by the news but glad he had more to go on. He was going to chat with Travis as soon as possible. He would share this with Dale and then gather up everything in order to approach him. His department had done all they could to find Tess, but this may have opened a door to her whereabouts.

The next day, Henry stopped by the feed store on the way over to discover that it was Travis's day off. Henry showed up at his parent's home.

"Who is it, Doris?" Tom asked.

"Looks like Henry. I wonder what he's doing out here."

Tom opened the door, "Hank, good to see you. Come on inside. Doris has the coffee on."

"Thanks, Tom. I see your heifer has gotten bigger."

"Yeah, she's a great addition to the family."

"Hello, Doris."

"Henry, always a pleasure to see you. Would you like some coffee?"

"Uh, no, thank you. Is Travis here?"

"Yes. He's in his room. Is everything okay?"

"Oh, sure. I just want to talk to him for a few minutes if that's okay with you two."

"We don't mind. It's the door on the left."

Henry had been thinking about this day for a while. He had all the clues he gathered from Dale and the person who came forward. It was coming together and he was hoping this would give him the breakthrough he was looking for.

"Travis." Henry announced as he knocked on the door.

Travis answered the door, slightly opening it. "Henry, what are you doing here?"

"Can we talk for a while?"

"I really can't. I have a lot of homework to do." Travis quickly shut the door. Henry pushed it back open.

"You can talk to me. I asked your parents and they were fine with it. Please, let me in and I will tell you why I'm here."

"Okay. We can talk."

Travis opened the door all the way and they both sat down. Travis was nervous, especially since he was in his parents' home and he didn't want them to know about Jess or Dan. Henry shut the door to have some privacy.

"I want to talk to you about Robbie."

"What about him?"

"You guys were pretty good friends, right? What do you know about the night he died?"

"Why are you asking me?"

"Because you know something. Who were you talking to that night?"

Travis hesitated and got up to look out the window that faced the back pasture.

"Come on, son. You might be afraid, but I want to help you."

"I don't believe you. Why would you want to help me?"

"We have a lot of evidence collected and we believe Robbie was killed by the same person who was in the Bronco with Tess, the missing reporter."

Travis's eyes got wide when he heard Tess's name. Henry was very good at reading body language and Travis was speaking loud and clear.

"I know you have information you're hiding. Should we talk at my office and bring Dale along?"

"No! Please don't involve anyone in this! I'll talk. I don't want my family to get hurt! I met a man a while ago who offered me a job to make some extra money. It was stupid. I did something I shouldn't."

"What did you do, Travis? There is a dead man and a woman missing. What have you got yourself into?"

"I know all about that! Robbie was my best friend. I begged him not to get involved. I think he went after him."

"Who went after him?"

"Henry, they will come after my family if I tell you."

"No, I will keep you safe. I just want to help you and Tess. Robbie shouldn't have had to die. If you care about him, you will do everything in your power to

148

help me find the men who did this. They can do this again to someone else. You don't want that on your conscience."

"I didn't kill him. I promise. Jess told me to get back home. I wasn't there when it happened. I tried to call Robbie to warn him but he didn't answer. I tried so many times to reach him."

"What did he tell you?"

"He shoved me hard on the shoulder and called me a coward."

"So, you didn't know Robbie's life was in danger that night?"

"Maybe. When I heard he died, I felt like it was my fault."

"Travis, you got trapped in a criminal's grip. I wish you would have come forward a long time ago."

"I was afraid they would hurt my dad and mom. They already killed Kyle's parents."

"What?! What did you just say?"

"Jess and Dan Masters set fire to Nathan's house. I thought you knew that."

"Travis, why would I know that? No one has come forth to tell me what they know about the fires. Listen, I want you to come down to the station and tell us everything you know in detail. I will let your parents know you are involved in an investigation and we will protect you and your family. Can you do that for me?"

"There's more you should know."

"You can save it for when we meet again." Henry got up walking towards the door.

"No, I have to tell you now." Suddenly, Henry stopped looking intrigued. He turned to look at Travis.

"Okay. What is it?"

"I know where Tess Charlton is."

Henry was in shock to hear that Travis was the only person who knew where Tess was. They searched for months and tried to interview some who may have been witnesses and they came up with nothing. Travis thought Henry knew everything. At that point, he felt it was important that he should tell him the whole story.

"Where is she? Travis, this is important. Her family has been looking for her for months. How could you keep this from the authorities?!"

"I didn't know what to do. I saw a flyer with her face on it and I went to Marion's to talk to her about it."

"She's at Marion's farm?"

"She's working there. She told me she doesn't know who she is. She said she lost all her memory and she only remembers what happened after the accident."

"So, she was in the car. We have evidence she was in the car with a man, an Edward Clemens."

"That's Dan."

"Edward is Dan Masters? He's got a very extensive record."

"When I met him, I didn't know that."

"He preyed on a young man like yourself to get what he wanted and now you don't know how to get away from him."

"Yes, he's still pushing me to burn more homes, but I said no. I have the money he paid me and I want to give it back. Actually, my dad has it. My mom found it in my drawer."

"Do they know?"

"No."

"I think they should know."

"You're right. It's time."

"Let's work on getting more from you before we spring it on them."

"What's going to happen to Tess?"

"We'll have to take this one slow. If she lost her memory, it may be too traumatizing to have her family and the press there. It could overwhelm her."

"I can't talk about this anymore. Let me know when you want me to meet with you and Dale."

"Thank you. You really did help. Don't have anything more to do with those men."

"I did tell Jess I didn't want to talk to them anymore. He said I have no choice and I am stuck with them because of what I know."

"We're going to change that. We'll be in touch."

Travis sat down on his bed consumed with guilt. Up until then, he had been a good kid and a reliable son. Recently, he was feeling like a failure and he needed to trust someone. He trusted Henry. This would be kept between them and they were going to do all they can to protect them from harm.

The next afternoon, Travis talked with the Sheriff and everything that was said was videotaped.

Doris and Tom were heartbroken that their son would do such a thing to his family. They realized that he was influenced and he was getting help. They appreciated his attitude when he told them he was willing to be punished for burning his grandfather's barn and anything else he was guilty for. Tom gave Henry the money for evidence. The parents wanted to do all they could to save their son and put him back on the right path. They observed Travis's remorse for the damage he shared in and reassured him of their love, despite what he had been through. The Sheriff ran a trace on Jess and Dan. They found old and new phone numbers with multiple addresses. San Diego detectives and police would trace where the men were. After giving his statement, Travis would be tried as a minor and have community service for two years. Henry planned to contact Kyle before returning Tess to her home.

Chapter 16

Who Do I Trust?

Kyle was finishing up the final touches on his house. It had turned into a cozy home standing proudly on the edge of his meadow. It's blue siding and white framing reflected Tess's preference. Above, perched two dormers with paned windows illuminating the upstairs rooms. Windows were placed strategically to let in natural light and capture the views of a spectacular horizon. Kyle focused on framing the sunset hues and changing colors of each season. A full porch invited visitors to the large door out front made of hardwood and glass. Blue Hydrangeas flanked the steps.

Inside still smelled of fresh wood and paint. A woven entry rug welcomed dirty boots and shoes. The floors and woodwork were finished walnut accented by area rugs and reupholstered antique chairs. A black stove sat on its stone hearth in the living room. Behind it stood a tan rock wall and a large pipe ascended through the ceiling. Antique corbels flanked each side of the entrance to the kitchen and dining area keeping some of the original flavor. They reminded him of his parents. He had rebuilt a large ash table for eight in front of the wooden French doors facing the forest.

Along the wall going upstairs hung photographs of Kyle and his family. From the pics saved in his phone he had them printed and framed. The rest of their family photos were destroyed. Whatever else he could salvage, he had restored or kept safe in a trunk. It sat at the top of the stairs as a bench.

In the larger bedroom was the new furniture that Tess helped pick out, except for the bed frame. Because she loved the one at Marion's, she found a similar one in the barn and painted it yellow. A handmade quilt given to Kyle after his parents died, was spread across the new mattress and cotton sheets. White sheers hung half-closed over the windows where breezes floated by.

Around the corner was the freshly tiled bathroom. Natural ash cabinets and white marble tops sat across from his bathtub. Kyle refinished the clawfoot he grew up with to look like new. It's underside was painted navy complimenting the soft blue towels laying across its edge.

The landscaping was designed and directed by Tess. Kyle could see it was where she belonged and naturally knew where to place the beauty and it looked perfect. Flowers, trees, and bushes had already attracted an array of butterflies and bees. In the trees in the backyard, she hung birdfeeders and a jar for the hummingbirds to get their sweet nectar. Near the kitchen window, honeysuckle climbed and Tess was humming as she trained wisteria to begin its ascent to the top of the pergola. Over the seasons, greenery would spread their leaves, touching one another, welcoming new life to the garden where flowers would drop seed and reproduce. Each day that Tess worked out there, she felt like there could be no other place to call home. The smell of fresh flowers inspired her to dream of planting larger flowerbeds with different varieties. Then she could pick her favorites and display them indoors on the table and nightstands. The ambiance turned out better than Kyle imagined. He realized that without Tess by his side, none of this would have been possible. It would have only been a house. But it was by far the prettiest house that ever rested in the country.

Back at Marion's farm, Tess started thinking about her last conversation with Travis. Would she be found out and have to leave the place she called home? In her mind, she knew no other place. She had learned how to ride horses, care for farm animals, cook, and work hard. Her loving heart motivated her to stay by the sick and helpless animals until Kyle could bring them back to health. She became close with each of them and she believed they loved her for her kindness. Most importantly, she had developed a deep love for the man who loved her. Nothing should get in the way of what they were building. Even though Tess still lived with Marion, Kyle's home was custom made for the two of them. Her future appeared beautiful.

Kyle was at his clinic after hours completing paperwork and organizing invoices. He was waiting on a shipment of supplies to arrive late in the day when he received a call.

"Henry, it's good to hear from you. What do I give the pleasure of this phone call?"

"I just wanted to come by and see you. Will you be there for a while?"

"Well, yes. I'm at my clinic here waiting on a delivery. Are you close by?"

"No, but I need to see you."

"Sounds serious."

"It could be."

"Could you fill me in?"

"I don't want to have a conversation on the phone. If it's okay with you, I'll swing by."

"You caught me on the right day. Usually I'm working on my house. Ryan and I have been hard at it."

"Ryan?"

"Oh, you haven't met her yet. She's Marion's hired hand. She really has a way with the animals and farm life."

"Are you romantically involved with her?"

"I am. She means everything to me. If it wasn't for her, I don't think I could've finished my home."

"I see. Well, I'll be by in about forty-five minutes."

"I'll wait for your arrival."

Kyle was clueless. He didn't know any information about Travis, Dan, or Jess. He wondered if it was something he did that sparked Henry's interest. So many thoughts were going through his mind. He decided to refocus on his duties at the clinic.

Marion was out with a friend for the afternoon while Tess managed the farm. Observing her over the months, she noticed she did well taking care of things even when Marion was away. Her friend was Edda Mae Wilkins, a retired nurse who recently relocated just down the road after living in Julian for many years.

"How are things with the new girl?"

"She's not so new anymore. She is a natural and a blessing on the farm. I'm glad she answered my ad."

"Have you heard anything more about the wrecked car or the missing reporter?"

"No. Is there any new information about it?"

"It seems that there was a man and a woman. Many of the folks think it was that missing woman. Her face is posted all over town."

"What do you mean?"

"They put up flyers trying to locate her."

"Do they have any clues as to where she is?" Marion pried.

"I don't know. I hate gossip and some of the people are too scared to share any news with me about what goes on there. That's why I left Julian. Word gets around in a small town."

"I agree." Marion was concerned about the flyers. She changed the subject as she poured the tea.

"Kyle's house is looking very nice."

"Oh, really? I wasn't aware he was fixing it. It's a shame some of the other homes are not so fortunate."

"I'm hoping that when the neighbors see the house, it will spur them on to come together and start repairing their town and the trust they lost."

"Lordy be," Edda Mae sighed. "It won't bring back Nathan and Cheryl."

"We sure had some happy memories. I miss them," Marion reminisced.

"I miss them too. We have sure been through a lot. My wish is for the town to be healed soon. Who knows, a miracle may surprise us all."

"That would be nice."

Marion couldn't help but think it was just a matter of time before Tess was discovered. She had come to love her like the daughter she always wanted. With everyone on alert, Marion thought about how much she would miss Tess if she suddenly left.

Henry parked in front of Kyle's clinic. He hated giving bad news as much as he loved solving mysterious situations. The way Kyle sounded on the phone; he could tell he was very fond of Tess. He wondered why he called her Ryan. Where did that name come from? Why would she change her name? Henry remembered something Travis said earlier; Tess lost her memory

157

after the accident. It sounded like she must have forgotten her name along with everything from her past. He tried opening the door but it was locked. There was a doorbell outside the building and he rang it. He could see Kyle coming to the door.

"Henry, just in time. I finished most of my work. Come in and take a seat."

"Thanks."

"So, what do you want to talk to me about? I have to admit, you got me worried."

"Can you tell me about Ryan?"

"Well, she moved out of the city to change her lifestyle for the country. Her full name is Ryan Lauren."

"Is that all you know about her?"

"With all due respect, why are you so concerned about Ryan?"

"I know more about her than you realize. Ryan Lauren is really Tess Charlton, a reporter." He paused watching Kyle's reaction. "We believe she was on an assignment to do a story about the Julian fires. We also guessed that she was trying to get information from a man named Dan Masters. From the evidence, they were both in the wreckage when they found the car. Neither of them have been found since."

"Dan Masters?! Why would she have anything to do with him? He hated my father. That can't be true."

"I'm afraid it is. There are posted flyers all over Julian. Her family has been looking for her. They want to bring her home."

"So, she's been lying to me?"

"I don't think that's the case. Did you know about her amnesia? From what we understand, she has no memory of Dan or anything before the accident."

"What?! How do you know that? I don't believe you."

"I know this is a shock, but this is the missing woman."

"Prove it!"

Henry pulled out her picture and handed it to him. Kyle stood up from his chair and paced. His thoughts were completely conflicted.

"Is she responsible for my parents' death?"

"We don't think so. We still have to interview her and she will have to be medically evaluated."

"Does she have to go home right now?"

"No. She can't leave immediately. She has amnesia. The shock could send her into a panic. She doesn't know anything about her life. We think her long term memory is gone. You and Marion were probably the best thing that ever happened to her."

"Suddenly, I don't trust her."

"You don't mean that."

"What am I supposed to feel? I can't imagine her with Dan."

"It may not be what you think." Henry was trying to reason with Kyle.

"You don't have any more evidence on why she was in the car with him? You don't know any more than this?"

"You and I know the same information. And Kyle, you can't tell her you know about her until we get this straightened out the right way."

"She should go home," he quietly reconciled.

"Kyle, why does this change how you feel about her? She still needs you. If you tell her, it may devastate her. Let us do this in a way that is best for Tess."

"Tess? I'm so used to calling her Ryan."

Kyle's eyes welled up with tears from confusion and betrayal. He didn't know what to think about Tess's identity. He had to regain his composure while in the presence of Henry.

"We are also going to tell Tess's parents that we found her. From there, we will form a plan on what to do. We have to approach this gently. Tess may have serious brain damage." He paused to let it sink in. After a moment, he continued, "I wish I had better news."

"Did they catch Dan yet?" Kyle was looking out the window.

"No. We are working on a trace to find him and Jess."

Kyle took a deep breath and regrouped his thoughts, "Thanks for coming by. I know none of this was your fault. You were just doing your job."

"I am doing more than my job, Kyle. I really care about you and everyone else who is affected by all this. I'll let myself out. Take care."

The news was just too painful. As Kyle drove back to his home for the night, he couldn't help replaying his beautiful memories with Tess. Then his thoughts would be sharply interjected by a woman with a different name. What else was she hiding? Was he foolish for trusting her? How could she hide her life from him? Then he remembered Henry's comment about her having serious brain damage. She did act a little lost, needing to be taught all sorts of little things, like using a rake and shovel, or the time she drove the pickup all over the field. It did make sense. But he was in love and his deep feelings were mixing him up. What if Tess was romantically involved with Dan, or worse, an accomplice? Kyle realized that he did not have all the facts and tried his best not to judge her.

Tess had been experiencing headaches and dizziness from time to time. She would stop and sit down or stare for a few seconds, until it passed. Tess did not connect it to her injury and would never see a doctor about it. She would not want to worry Marion about the episodes, either. She had come to terms with her memory loss and believed she would never get it back. When flashes of memory surfaced, she panicked and longed to be in the arms of Kyle, for comfort. Marion noticed she wasn't always herself. Increasing forgetfulness and lack of balance concerned her. She decided to have a talk with a local doctor about Tess's symptoms. She would still honor her secret and not mention Tess. After calling Dr. Samuels, Marion drove to talk to him at his office.

"Thank you for meeting with me."

"It sounded like an emergency. Are you feeling okay, Marion?"

"Yes. What I want to talk to you about is not about me. I have a young friend who has some symptoms."

"What's the problem?"

"Well, she fell and hit her head and is now experiencing some memory loss and night terrors. She is not as steady on her feet these days and has little long-term memory. What could be wrong?"

"A brain injury like that is very serious. She's fortunate she is alive and able to function. Will you bring her in and let me help her?"

"She's a bit stubborn about doctors. Will it get worse?"

"She might stabilize, but she could still become disoriented by panicky thoughts of past memories or worse, experience a seizure or blackout."

"What should I do?"

"She should get an MRI to see if there is any swelling or to determine what kind of brain injury is causing her symptoms. Marion, whoever this is with these issues, needs to seek medical attention sooner than later."

"I agree. I will talk her into getting help. Thank you Dr. Samuels."

Marion concern for Tess grew stronger. It looked like she should give up on hiding and go get treatment.

After she walked into her home, Marion noticed Tess sleeping on the couch. She walked over and swept the hair away from her eyes. Her maternal love impelled her to protect Tess's life beyond irreparable damage. She felt responsible for her safety and knew they needed to have a serious conversation.

"Oh, hello, Marion. What time is it?" Tess said as she opened her eyes.

"It's after three. How are you feeling?"

"I had that headache again, so I thought I'd sleep it off. They come and go."

"I want to talk to you about something that has me quite troubled."

"What is it?"

"I went to talk to my doctor today and asked him about your symptoms."

"You told him about me?" Tess sat up.

"No. I just asked some questions about your symptoms. He doesn't suspect anything about you or your whereabouts. Tess, this is important. You may have a serious brain injury. You should be glad you're still alive with all you've been through."

"What are you saying?" she questioned nervously.

"I think you should tell Dale about what you know and have him find your family. Because your life may be in danger, you need to get some professional help."

"No, no. I can't leave! Did I do something wrong?"

Marion put her hand on her cheek, "I want you to be safe. But sweetie, you have not been feeling well and I care about you too much to see you suffer."

"Somedays I feel okay, other times I have thoughts that I don't understand. I've been hoping it would get better with time."

"I can't force you to get help. You need to think about it and take care of yourself before something serious happens. I will always be here when you need me."

"Travis knows about me."

"When did this happen?"

"I don't remember the exact time. He showed me a picture of my face and my name."

"So, you remember your name?"

"He said my name is Tess Charlton. I used to be a reporter and everyone is looking for me. But I can't go back to the way things used to be. This has changed everything and I'm afraid I won't even know my family."

"That's a possibility, but I'm sure they care for you and are probably worried."

Just then, Kyle turned down the drive toward the house. Marion looked out the window.

"It's Kyle. He must be here to drop off the ointment for Bessie."

"I want to go talk to him."

"Honey, now that everyone is searching for you, please give it some thought. Your safety matters to me."

"I will."

Tess ran out to meet Kyle.

"Kyle, I'm so glad to see you. Can you stay a while?" smiled Tess.

He did not look excited to see her.

"No. I need to get back to the clinic. I have to be in surgery today."

"Okay. Are you alright?"

"Who's Tess?" Kyle blurted against the request from Henry.

"Where did you hear that name?"

"It doesn't matter where I heard it. Tell me who you are."

"I wish I could tell you the whole story about me and who I was. I am Tess Charlton."

"Why didn't you tell me what happened to you?"

"I just couldn't. Everything was so confusing and I lost my life and all I worked hard for. Now that you know, what does this mean for us?"

"There are times when I have trouble trusting. I think if you knew something, you should have been honest enough to tell me about it. Do you have anything you want to tell me?"

"I don't know anything. What do you want me to say? I lost my memory."

"And Dan? What were you doing with him? I can't even look at you right now! How could you do this to me?"

"You think this was my fault?! I have no control over what happened that day I woke up from the crash. I don't remember who Dan is." Tess was upset when Kyle questioned her motives.

"That was the answer I expected to hear from you."

"What does that mean? What are you getting at? I love you and that's what counts, nothing else."

"Honesty and trust make love last. If you can't be honest with me, then I think we should just go our separate ways!"

"I don't want to be without you!" Tess cried.

"When you are ready to tell me more about yourself and why you came here, I will listen. Right now, I can't be around you. Here is the medicine for Bessie. I have to go."

"Kyle, I'm not sure what you want from me."

He couldn't look at her. "I want to trust you and it kills me inside that I can't. What happened to my family has devastated me. To know he was with you in that car sickens me. I suggest you go home and leave me alone."

"No! I was in the dark until you came into my life. I can't have you leave me like this!" She held his arm, begging him not to go.

"Go home, Tess, if that is your real name."

Kyle pushed her hand away and got into his truck without looking back. She was left there in tears. She wanted to tell him everything she remembered but the trauma was too much to relive. Losing Kyle gave her one less reason to stay. Marion was probably right. She had a lot to process and her heart was just broken. Lost and alone, she slowly walked into the house with her head down. Marion tried to talk to her, but she just went to her room to cry.

She loved Kyle's house, the memories they built, and the love they felt for each other. To think of starting life over, felt overwhelming and scary. She knew she could never go back to being a reporter. But what about her parents, her friends, her past? So many questions were jumping around in her mind. Deciding

165

to return home might not be such a bad idea. Was that really what she wanted? Her existing memory said to stay, but her lost memory gave her reason to return home.

Chapter 17

Leave The Light On For Me

Henry had been working overtime gathering more information about Tess's case. He was finding the best way to tell her parents she was alive and give them the whole story about what happened to their beloved daughter. He located their address to tell them in person. Henry was an experienced detective. He had been educated on how to deliver news, ask pertinent questions, and get good answers. This, however, was a different scenario than any he had been trained for. His extra research would pay off.

Henry stopped at the curb and looked at the home of Dean and Sara Charlton. He knew as soon as he told them about Tess, they would want her brought home. Getting out of his car, he approached the door knowing he was about to change their world. He wanted to get this family back on their feet. They deserved the comfort of knowing she was safe.

"Hello, can I help you?" Dean asked.

Henry showed him his ID badge.

"My name is Henry Calhoun. I am a detective working on your daughter's case. I'd like to talk to you."

"Please, come in. This is my wife, Sarah."

"Nice to meet you," Henry said formally.

Sarah's face was concerned. Henry couldn't help but notice how Tess's picture looked like her parents.

Dean pointed to a chair and began with his questions, "What do you know about her? We did get some results back that said she was in a car with someone. We just couldn't understand why they couldn't find her."

"Is she still alive?" Sarah chimed in.

"Your daughter is alive and safe."

"What?! Tess, she's okay? Why isn't she with you? Where is she?"

"I know you have lots of questions. Just give me a minute to explain. She's staying with a wonderful friend at a farm who is taking good care of her."

"We'd like to go get her and bring her home," Dean announced.

"There's something you need to know about Tess first. When she was in that accident, she was injured. She doesn't have any long term memories. I don't think she would know who either of you are if she was here. Marion is doing a good job caring for her."

"Marion may have good intentions, but she is our daughter."

"I realize that. She may suffer shock from your presence or worse, with the press. Brain injuries like hers can be scary for anyone who loses their memory. I think she should be approached tenderly, so as to not panic her."

"If we can't see her, what can we do?" asked Sarah

"There isn't much to do while we are still investigating. We are still uncovering some dangerous people, including the man who was in the car with her."

"Why was she in the car with him? I still don't understand why she would be with a man like that."

"We think she was trying to get information about the fires. She has no recollection that she was ever a reporter. It's going to take time for her to regain bits of her life back. That will take patience on your part. Do you think you can have the patience to do that?"

"We'll do whatever it takes to help Tess. How long will it be until we can see her?"

"I'm going to talk to her and try to encourage her to come home. She may resist for a while. We just have to have hope that she will decide what is best for her."

Henry unfolded the story about Tess, Marion, Kyle, and Travis. He related their fears of Dan, who was still out there, a master at evasion. Dean and Sarah were fearful for their daughter. They would have to trust and wait until the time was right.

As Henry was getting into his car, he got a text message from Dale.

"I need to talk to you. Jess came into the station and is confessing."

Henry called immediately. "Dale, what do you mean he confessing?"

"He told us everything. He even confessed who killed Robbie Carnes. He hired an attorney to help him with his case. We have him in custody right now."

"I didn't see that coming. What made him come in?"

"After informing Dan that he didn't want to deal with him any longer and he wanted out of their deal, Dan threatened him pretty bad. I guess it really scared him and he thought he would be protected if he confessed. Jail was his best option."

"So, where's Dan?"

"We don't know. This guy has so many aliases and we only know him as Dan or Edward."

"I think he's going to go after Tess. He's not the kind of guy to give up. He's already lost two of his partners in crime."

"Henry, where are you at now?"

"I'm in San Diego. I told Tess's parents where she is. I'm on the way back now. I'll see you as soon as I get back. Thanks for the news."

Henry was formulating a plan while driving. He had to convince Tess to return home. Jess was behind bars and probably knew more than he let on. Dan needed to be caught. It was time to finish this case before anyone else got hurt. He had high hopes for that town to get back on their feet.

Henry arrived at the station to question Jess further. After reading the original interview, he entered the local jail where he was held until his trial.

"I want to talk to you. You gave us some information already that I have scanned through. There are a few more puzzle pieces we need to wrap this up. I hope you're ready to tell me everything."

"What choice do I have? If you want to know where Dan is, I don't know. He lays low and he's hard to find."

"Are you sure about that?"

"I confessed, didn't I?"

"What do you know about the woman who was in the car with him?"

"She was asking him questions and he told me he was going to get rid of her. He had to do it because I told him I wouldn't go that far. He killed Kyle's parents in that fire and I knew if I kept working for him, I'd end up in prison right next to him. I guess that's where I'm ending up anyhow. Dan has a way of ruining anyone who comes near him. I just want a chance to reform my life. If I knew where he was, I'd tell you."

"You did the right thing getting away from him. You're biggest mistake was being an accomplice to killing an innocent reporter. Travis is paying the hard way too."

"He's smart enough to get away while he is still young. I wish I had that chance."

"I would suggest you clear the air and tell your attorney everything. That might help your case and how much time you spend in corrections."

"Yeah, I got it." He paused. "Hey, Hank. I'm so sorry for all the losses I've caused."

"Just get your life together."

Dean talked to his attorney about their daughter's situation. He agreed with Henry. But, not having her there with them was all they could think about. They wanted to rush in and take her home and worry about the consequences later, but they had to think responsibly.

Marion wasn't expecting Henry to show up when he did. She could see his desire to make things right as soon as possible. She needed to get medical help and assistance from her parents.

"Good to see you, Henry."

"Hi, Marion. Hope you are doing well. How is Tess? Can I talk to her?"

"So, you know about her? She may not want to talk right now. Kyle just broke up with her and she is devastated."

"Do you know why they broke up?"

"No. He came by and they were talking outside. Next thing I knew, she came in crying and went upstairs."

"It's crucial I speak to her. Her parents finally learned that she's here."

171

"I tried to encourage her to go home earlier. I am watching her health worsen each day. She needs help."

"Marion, if she won't go home, I need you to work with me. I know you love Tess."

"Yes. Anything for her to be well again."

Marion let Henry inside.

"Tess, come down please."

Near the bottom of the stairs, Tess saw Henry and stopped.

"Who is this?"

"This is Henry Calhoun. He wants to help you."

"You called him to come here?"

"No. He came by on his own to talk to you."

"I don't want to talk." She started to go back upstairs.

"Tess, I am a detective and I know all about you and the man who was with you in the car. I want you to trust me. You are not in trouble. I'm here to help you." She turned to look at him.

"How can you help me? I have no life, no one."

"Come sit with us and let's talk," Henry offered.

"It's alright, Tess," Marion encouraged. "I'll be right here."

She came down and sat near Marion.

"First, I want to say how sorry I am that you were in the accident with Dan. It must have been very traumatic. I know you are having trouble with your memory and I will not judge you, good or bad. Whatever you can recall is okay with me. Now, what can you think of that will help put this man away for good and never hurt anyone again."

"I don't know anything about him. Sometimes, I have thoughts of being in that car with him driving too fast. He wanted to take me someplace. I don't know how the car was wrecked. When I woke up, the man next to me was still unconscious."

"Do you remember anything else?"

"No. Until I met Travis, I didn't know anything about myself. I don't want to think about my losses any longer. Kyle knows a little about me."

"Yes, and so do your parents."

Tess was surprised and looked at Marion. "My parents?"

"I met with them and they want you to come home."

"I was thinking about going home now that Kyle no longer wants me. But I don't want to leave Marion." She noted anxiously.

"No, don't worry about old Marion. I'll be fine. I want you have a good life and besides, your family loves you."

Henry calmed her, "I don't want to pressure you into something you're not ready for. But you let me know when you want to go home and I will help."

"Can I go back to my room? I think I need to rest."

"Alright."

Tess did have a lot to think about. She wanted to phone Kyle again and tell him how much she missed him. So many times she called with no response.

Sitting alone in his new home felt cold and pointless. In the dimness of his living room, the wood stove warmed him as he stared at its flickering flames. His hands held a picture of his parents before they died. Kyle couldn't stop thinking about her. His mind kept pardoning Tess for her memory loss. However it nagged him to know she was involved with the man responsible for his parents death. His heart pained. He was almost sure that Dan had something to do with his parents' death and for Tess to be with him during the accident, was not coincidence. Why couldn't he forgive her and move on, believing she had nothing to do with it? He looked out at the moonlit garden Tess planted and it made him emotional. He just couldn't bring himself to take her back. The next morning, he grabbed his keys and headed to Marion's.

"What are you doing here?" Tess asked surprised.

"I wanted to say how sorry I am for the last time we spoke. I just have to say that I have thought about it until my brain hurts. I, I can't take you back. There is far too much pain."

"You don't have to worry about that anymore. I've decided to go home. My parents' are coming to get me today and you will never have to see me again. I know you think I had something to do with Dan and even if I told you I didn't, you wouldn't believe me. I wish I could remember why I was there with him. I can't change that. I still cannot understand why you can't accept that from me, the woman who never knew love before. You really hurt me!"

"Maybe I will feel different in time."

"I'm not waiting for you to have faith in me. I've lost everything and I may never get back who I was. I wanted you to love me for who I am, who you fell in love with. You chose to believe what you wanted."

"I'll miss you, Tess. I never wanted it to end like this. I just want to get rid of this ache I feel losing my parents. It's like they died all over again."

"That's all you have to say? I wanted my life to include you and it sounds like that will never happen."

174

Kyle bowed his head and walked to the other end of the porch.

Tess went back up the steps of the shaded porch waiting for her parents to arrive. She was going to leave the farm just like she arrived, with only the clothes on her back.

Hours later, a car turned off of the main road and approached slowly. It was Dean, Sarah, and their attorney. Tess stood fearfully on the porch while Marion stepped outside to welcome the visitors. As they got out of the car, Marion and Kyle watched Tess's mother weeping as she walked towards her daughter. Dean followed closely behind.

"Hello, I'm Dean Charlton. Henry said you were the one who took care of our daughter. We are forever in your debt for your kindness. Thank you."

Marion replied, "No need for that. I was happy to be here for her. Tess is a remarkable survivor. We all just fell in love with her."

"We? Who else took care of her?"

"Kyle James," she pointed.

Dean turned to shake his hand. "Thank you, son."

"I'm glad I was there for her." Kyle whispered as his sad eyes turned to look at Tess.

The parents slowly approached Tess and went to hug her. She hesitated for a moment and then forced herself to hug back. It was far from natural.

"Oh, honey, we are so glad you're coming home," Sarah said secretly hoping the sound of her voice would magically unlock all of Tess's memory.

"Can we just go now?" Tess pled with sorrow in her voice. She turned and hugged Marion. "Goodbye, Marion. I'll miss you."

"We can always keep in touch. They will take good care of you. Love you, Tess."

"I love you too."

She glanced over, "Goodbye, Kyle."

Kyle could just wave. He wanted to run into her arms, but he didn't fit into her new life with her parents. A deeper sadness came over him as he watched her leave. He would never see her in the barn observing the animals adore her. He would never hear her laughter or see her smile again. He couldn't get himself to live in his new home that Tess helped fix and put her touches to. He dreamed of a future when she would come back. He didn't know how long, but he needed time to recover.

He sat in his driver's seat and started the truck. He looked back as he closed the door. The farm would not be the same. Marion could see tears glistening on his cheek. As his dusty taillights neared the end of the drive, her dog reached his nose up under her hand wanting affection.

"Good boy, old Codger," Marion gently said.

Kyle was unlocking the clinic the next morning. His vet techs had not arrived when Henry walked in.

"Why are you here? More questions? I don't have any more information for you," Kyle said sarcastically as he was looking through the drawers of his file cabinet. He then slammed the drawer.

"I'm not here to grill you, Kyle. Something's been on my mind all night. Why would you do that to Tess? I know you still love her."

"What did I do? She needed to go home."

"No, she needed you. You had the chance to support her and help her through her pain and confusion, but you chose to cast her aside when she needed you."

"What else was I supposed to do?! I thought I was done with Dan Masters and now he is back in my life again? I loved her, Henry. To think about her in that car with him, kills me inside. It's too much."

"She had nothing to do with the death of your parents. She was doing her job trying to bring justice for her friend, Robbie. Dan was trying to kill her and we think she was being kidnapped. She may have caused the accident to get away from him, who knows? For you to think so shallow and believe she was coerced into a crime, is something I can't fathom."

"I don't know what to say! I can't stop seeing her with him."

"You need to restore your relationship. It will also help both of you to heal from the trauma. I believe she still loves you. To be honest, I don't know why she would forgive you except that she has a heart of gold. You know she would have done anything for you."

Henry turned and stormed out of his office. Kyle felt the anxiety flow through his body thinking about letting the woman he loved get away. How could he hurt her that way? His deeper fear was that she would never return. Every day he would leave the light on, hoping to be surprised by her walking back into his life. But she never did. As the season drifted by, Kyle carried on...without Tess.

Each day he spent time with Marion, he would sit in the barn and pet Annabelle visualizing Tess beside them. The torture reopened wounds instead of healing no matter how much time went by. Henry's words continued to ring in his ears. It was not Tess's fault. His disbelief may have ruined his chances for a fulfilling life with the beautiful person who put life into him. Kyle was left with conflicting thoughts and he knew it was his own fault for misjudging. He took to heart Marion's encouragement to be happy for Tess getting healthy and reconnecting with her parents. Kyle would always be in love with her. He realized that

nothing would change that. What would change his
life would be the return of Dan Masters.

Chapter 18

The Journey of Tess Charlton

The paper announced their missing reporter, who had become quite well-known by that time, had finally returned. Those who adored her were not able to welcome her back personally. It would have overwhelmed her. Tess stayed at her parents' home for a few months. A visit to the neurologist to assess her condition was scheduled by her parents. It was determined that she had suffered a severe concussion and developed a subdural hematoma. With that kind of injury, additional symptoms tended to surface weeks after the incident. It was recommended that Tess have surgery as soon as possible to relieve some of the pressure against her brain. The severity of the trauma, related to the accident may have contributed to slow recovery. Weekly evaluations concluded that her physical health was good but did not provide hope about her amnesia. It was expected to be fairly permanent.

She was quiet at home, still getting to know her parents. As advised, they avoided showing pictures of her or her job. She was slowly warming up to her mother. Connecting her to those times in her thoughts when she could hear her call her name.

Her parents noted that she remembered everything about Kyle. She revealed how much he meant to her and what love meant, even though it was a new experience. He still held her heart and she hoped he was thinking about her in the same way. Some of her memories sounded childlike and innocent such as when she relived being with Marion and her animals. Tess would have moments of high anxiety with intrusive thoughts. It scared her parents at first, but the doctor put her on some medication to calm her.

Each morning she would awaken thinking she was still at the farm and missed the animals welcoming her to feed them. It just wasn't the same. She would ask each day, "when can I see Marion again?" Her mother didn't know what to say. She didn't want to lose her daughter again and the thought of her going back scared her.

After several weeks, Tess was offered an opportunity to see her apartment. Her parents were still paying her rent in hopes that she would return soon.

When they opened the apartment door, Tess slowly went through looking around without recognizing anything in the room. She came into the kitchen and noticed the espresso machine. She put her hand on it and turned to Margo.

"What is this?"

"It's your espresso machine. It dispenses coffee. It used to be your favorite drink."

"Marion gave me a coffee once. I didn't like it."

"Now that you are in here, how are you feeling, honey?" Sarah asked.

"This place doesn't look like me. I don't think I can stay here."

"We can change some things to make it more comfortable for you," Margo encouraged.

"I miss the farm. Marion used to make me pancakes and my favorite eggs. I miss the animals, the farmhouse, the barn."

"We know you miss her. Have you called her?"

"No. I'm afraid I'll hear her sad voice." Tess looked at her mother and requested, "Can I have a few minutes with Margo?"

"Sure. I'll be outside."

"Tess, it's so good to have you back. I was so worried about you. Digby wanted to come see you but he wants to give you some time."

"My boss? Do they call him Digs sometimes?"

"Yes."

"His name used to pop up in my head while I was away."

"Really?"

"Yes. I would have brief thoughts about my past and sometimes I would get a memory back. What is my relationship with you?" Margo's eyes turned sad as Tess asked.

"We were good friends and I was your assistant. We worked together all the time. Do you know about your career as a reporter?"

"No. It's getting easier to ask questions. I have no idea what I actually did before the accident."

"What was it like living up there when you lost your memory?"

Tess's eyes sparkled, "It was beautiful. Being there in the open fields and watching the meadow dance for me. It was breathtaking. Sunrises and sunsets filled me. During that time, I fell in love."

"What's his name?"

"Kyle James. He's someone I will never forget. He and I did so much together and we got close working with the animals and rebuilding his house. Then he broke up with me the day I left."

"Why?"

"I think it had something to do with the man that was in the car with me. He may have killed Kyle's parents in a fire. He was just too hurt over so much and it seemed like a trigger for him. I want to call him and go see him, but I know he can't change his mind about me."

"Tess, you mentioned taking care of animals. I couldn't even convince you to get a dog. How did you take care of a whole farm full of animals?"

"I learned," Tess chuckled.

"You are different and it won't change how much I love you. I would love to get to know the new Tess Charlton."

"I'm not good company for anyone at the moment. I seem to have a long way to go before I am better."

"I can wait. I will always be around and I got your back. If you don't want to live here, we can find a place to stay that suits you."

"I'd like that."

The two women talked and Margo saw Tess's smile come back. Margo never lost hope that Tess would find her way back home. Their friendship was slowly being built back and Tess liked her company.

Sarah and Dean found a new apartment for Tess. It was getting easier for her to live on her own. Because she was unable to hold a job, her parents helped pay for her basic expenses. She continued seeing a therapist to help her cope with her confusing recurring thoughts.

On Margo's day off, she took Tess shopping. They ended up at the book store two blocks away. Tess loved reading more than watching TV, one thing Marion refused to have. She found the section where they kept animal care and below it on the bottom shelf were oversized coffee table books. She was attracted to the photography of meadow and mountain scenery. Margo looked on as Tess flipped through the pages smiling at each picture. She could see how much her friend missed that life. She purchased three books on farm life.

In her new apartment, Tess looked in the mirror. The scar from the accident was a constant reminder causing her to tear up. She recounted Kyle touching her face tenderly when she mentioned it no longer hurt. Gazing into his eyes meant everything and it held what was in store for them. It never crossed her mind to leave him or the place she called home. He was her home. Those close to her could see she was happier before her new life in the city.

While Tess was home one evening talking on the phone with her mother, she heard a knock.

"Sorry, Mom. I have to go. Someone is here."

Looking through her window, she saw an older man waving at her. She opened the door a few inches.

"Hello?"

"Tess, it's Digby. I'm sorry I came without notice. I was on my way home and I thought I would give you these."

He handed her some fresh flowers.

"Oh, thank you. I love these. Would you like to come in?"

"Thank you."

"Margo told me a little about you. I'm sorry I don't remember you."

"You've been through a lot. I understand. It's not the same without you at the newspaper."

183

"I'm not ready to come see the place yet. Margo said, everyone wants to see me. What was I like working for the paper?"

"The greatest reporter that ever lived. You were the best I ever hired. Everything seems different now that you're not there."

"I'm so sorry."

"Oh, there's nothing to be sorry for. I'm the one who is sorry."

"I must have made a mistake that I can't remember. I'm trying to make the best of it."

"I know you were doing this for Robbie. You made a sacrifice for someone who was special to you. That is a part of you that memory loss won't take away. You're still Tess and that's what I love about you and your drive to do the best job possible. I will miss that part of you."

Digby continued to express his feelings about losing Tess.

"When you went missing, I felt like the life was ripped from me. I could see the pain in your father's face each time we talked about you. I felt that too. Maybe someday, you will have that drive to return and you could come back to the paper."

"I appreciate that you would like me to give it a try. I can't think about that right now."

"You are missed by all the staff."

"Thank you, Digby, for everything you did to help me be the best I could be. I'm sure you were a good support for me. I should have listened to you and not covered the fires.

"That's not who you are. The passion is inside you, Tess. You were always determined to go for your goal.

That's what I love about you. We all wish we had that drive. Never let that go."

"I hope to find it again soon."

It was a profound loss for Digby Stone. She was not dead, but it was nearly the same. Losing Tess was heartbreaking. As he left her home, he had to wipe his eyes thinking about memories of working with his favorite reporter. Even though she wasn't the same, he still loved her. Digby never had children and having Tess around was the closest he would have to his own daughter. He spent a lot of time with her parents and did all he could to comfort them waiting for her. It turned out to affect more than Tess's parents. A large number of readers and fans of the paper wrote in sympathy notes and posted online. Digby's long-time reporter, Charlie, wrote a touching article about Tess's return and the positive reaction of the community.

The words read like this:

Charlie Haskins

Reporter for The News Day

We are honored to have Tess Charlton back safe in her hometown with her friends and family. Tess was a phenomenal reporter and a gifted mentor for those who wanted to learn from her. She wanted justice for Robbie Carnes and she desired to teach young reporters how to cover a good story. As you may be aware, she was reporting a pivotal piece and after surviving an accident, she lost her long-term memory. We didn't lose a great reporter; we gained a gifted human being who made the ultimate sacrifice for a fellow journalist. Some of those involved in the fires have been apprehended, inspiring the town to mend and rebuild trust. Tess enjoyed the beautiful meadows and mountains surrounding the Julian area. Our city of San Diego along with neighboring communities are proud of Tess and her remarkable efforts. She created a legacy for anyone who has the passion to work hard for their dream. We welcome her back home and wish the best for her with a speedy recovery.

More letters poured in about the article and some of the towns in the San Diego County were glad that Julian could once again be a safe place to grow and raise their families.

Each day Tess looked at her phone, hoping to get a call from Kyle. As she stepped out of the shower, her phone rang. She noticed Kyle's name on the ID. It had been several months since she last talked to him at Marion's.

"Hello," she answered apprehensively.

"Tess, it's Kyle."

"How are you? I haven't heard from you in so long."

"I wanted to call so many times, but I just couldn't do it after we parted. I wanted you to make a life for yourself and I didn't want to get in your way."

"I'm getting better. Why are you calling me?"

"I miss you. I still haven't moved into my house. It's not the same without you here."

"I know. I miss you and Marion. I think I'm still recovering from saying goodbye. "

"Do you ever think about coming back?"

"I'm not sure when or if it will ever happen. You hurt me and left me without answers."

"I know. I have to say, I'm so sorry for that."

"You never did tell me why you called."

"I just wanted to see how you're feeling."

"That's it?" she asked quietly. "Nothing else?"

186

There was silence on his end and she waited patiently for him to speak.

"I guess not. I know you'll eventually get your old life back without me. Take care, Tess."

She said, 'I love you,' as Kyle hung up the phone.

She realized he did not hear it and sadness filled her. Hearing his voice was crushing and she wished everything would go back to the way it was when they were together.

Walking through his home, Kyle thought about the things he should have said to Tess. Why was he holding back? His life could never be the same and he knew he had a measure of pride to overcome. Entering her favorite bedroom upstairs, he glanced at her throw pillows all stacked poetically. He did not remember seeing the yellow one. Marion embroidered Tess's name on its front and flowers around the edges. When Kyle lifted it, he discovered a handwritten note underneath. His name was on one side. He slowly picked it up and unfolded it. It was written by Tess.

My Dearest Kyle,

There are so many things I don't understand about my life or myself. I have been lost and afraid until I found you. I try to imagine my younger days and what I loved about my life. Without a memory, I felt like I was slowly fading away until I suddenly fell in love. With a broken mind, I remember all of the many things I loved about you. You truly love your land, your animals, and your waving meadows.

I have forgotten all I used to be except for the love I have for you. That is a memory that cannot blow away like petals in the wind. I close my eyes and envision a wonderful thought; a beautiful flower beaten by heavy raindrops during a storm. Instead of looking up to see the rain that keeps it alive, it looks down, almost lying on the ground without hope. When the sun comes out, the drops of rain are like

187

tears trickling down onto the ground, comforting the tired flower. Relief finally comes to rescue what was beautiful. The petals can now hold themselves up and stand straight knowing there is survival after a storm. Visitors of comfort pass by. The butterfly and bee land to say, "we are glad that you are alive." Beauty comes in many forms, but it doesn't have to be destroyed or weakened by tragedy.

I may be slightly broken, but not beyond hope. My strongest fear is to lose you. I cry at times, amazed that despite my pain, I can conquer the troubles around me. I am made new each day. Who I used to be is gone and I miss her. She used to belong to me and now she is just who I was. Please, my love, forgive me for what I must do. I hope someday you will welcome me back into your world of devotion and love. Keep the light on in your heart and I will use it to guide me, to guide me back home. I love you, Tess.

Kyle tightened his grip and let his eyes drift out the window. He was amazed by the poetic flow in each line pouring out of her honest heart. He knew she was the best thing that happened to him. Reading her desires made him feel more guilty for letting her go. Nothing had been the same. She had a way of making the sunsets brighter and the evenings memorable. Kyle's smile returned as he realized how much he still loved her. Why was he so afraid to take her back?

Downtown, Tess asked if she could spend the night at her parents' house. She realized she needed a break for comfort amidst all the recent changes. Their home was full of family memories. She wandered the house looking around for anything familiar. For a while, images came in and out that made little sense. Whatever Tess had was nearly gone and she was coming to terms with that. She studied the photos on the wall, especially the group shots of her and her parents. Those were apparently special times shared with friends and family. She still couldn't recognize anyone. Sarah had taken Tess's photo albums and scrapbooks from her home to protect from shock. When Tess went into her old bedroom, she found them near the nightstand. Opening the first page, she noticed articles written by her that were cutout and pasted. A few pages later, she found honors earned for excellence in journalism and reporting. Continuing through it, all she could see was hard work and it disappointed her. That part of her was gone forever. Her mother peered into the room.

"Tess, what are you doing in here?" she asked kindly.

"I just thought I would see where I used to be. I wanted to remember what it was like to be a reporter. I must have been too busy to have a real life. It hurts to think that one mistake caused it to all go away." She covered her eyes and began to cry, feeling responsible for the accident and her current condition.

"Tess, you are the bravest person I know. You have always been passionate about journalism. It was built in you to go chase your dream. That accident may have saved you in a sense."

"How so?"

"They suspected that the man in the car with you was going to end your life. I think you did what you had to do to save your own life. I miss who you used to be. But sweetie, most of all, I will always love the person who is here with me right now."

"Thanks. I can't stop thinking about Kyle."

"Why don't you talk to him?"

"There's just too much pain in his heart. I think we both need time to heal. Since surgery, I have been feeling better. I don't have as many headaches and rarely get that spacey aura. I sometimes wonder, when will I stop feeling lost? Kyle made me feel like nothing bad ever happened. I loved being on the farm with him. But the issues with Dan are still lingering around and he can't get it out of his mind."

"What is it that you really want to do?"

"I'm afraid to tell you."

"Oh, honey. You can say how you feel. What do you want?"

She took a breath and looked up at her mother's eyes.

"I want to go back to Marion's farm and be with Kyle."

Sarah was torn, thinking about losing her little girl again. But she knew the right thing to say.

"You are a grown woman. You have always went for what you wanted. If being with Kyle will make you happy, then you should go do what you must."

Tess held her mother. Sarah touched her hair realizing that Tess was telling the truth about her happiness. All the memories she held close as a mother were just that, memories. Tess's heart would never be a reporter again. Even if she tried, it would not be fulfilling. Both Dean and Sarah didn't want her to leave but wanted what was best for their daughter.

Enough time had passed since Kyle's last conversation with her and she had no idea if he had moved on or met someone else.

Tess's parents drove her to the farm to say their goodbyes there. Codger was on the porch giving a bark announcing guests and Marion's face appeared in the window.

"Well, I'll be. Tess!"

After embracing, both women were elated to be reunited again.

"I needed to come home. If you will have me, I want to be part of this life with you."

"What about Kyle?" Marion asked.

"He doesn't know I'm here."

Dean came onto the porch to talk to Marion.

"We want Tess to be happy with her new life. We think of you as family and we know you will take good care of her."

"You are always welcomed as my guest and family."

"Mom, Dad, thank you both for letting me come. I promise I'll call and you can come visit anytime."

"We love you, Tess." Dean held his daughter tightly and wiped tears from her face.

"This isn't goodbye. Go have another adventure. I love you so much," Sarah said as she released Tess from her hug.

She waved until the car drove out of sight. Codger followed them into the house and laid on the kitchen floor. Marion sat at the kitchen table with Tess.

"This has certainly been quite an adventure already," Marion commented.

"It sure has."

"I left your old room just how you like it." Marion said with a smile on her face.

"Thank you."

Marion could see the expression on Tess's face and how much she wanted to talk to Kyle. She was holding back and Marion had to give her a nudge.

"We could sit here and talk about ourselves with a cup of tea, but I can see something more interesting behind your eyes. So tell me, when are you going to call Kyle?"

"I can't talk to him right now. I need to think it through first. I had a lot to think about while I was away. Maybe he doesn't want me anymore. I don't want to be surprised by that kind of news."

"Well, the only way to find out is to go talk to him."

"Why am I afraid to go to him? I know I'm still in love with him. It's been a long time since we last saw each other. A lot has changed and he could feel differently."

"Now, you mustn't feel that way. You have to have hope. Everyone says you used to have such a passion for reporting. You still have passion in you. It's there, you just have to find it."

"Will you take me to him? I want to go up to the house."

"I would be honored to take you up there. I think you'll find a very good surprise."

"I hope you're right."

Marion parked in the shade of an oak tree outside of Kyle's house. She nodded to Tess reassuring her it was okay and asked, "Are you ready?"

"No. I'm a little nervous."

"Go to him. Find that passion."

Tess walked up to the front door. Inside, Kyle could see a woman standing behind his glass door.

"Tess. I'm surprised to see you."

"Marion brought me. I want to talk."

"Really? I haven't heard from you in months."

"I had surgery to help repair my brain and I have been in treatment to help me feel better. You should know that my memory loss is permanent. The memories I built here; right here with you are never going to disappear. I don't think I can live my life without you.

No matter how you feel about me, I'm here to stay and I will always be in love with you. I want you to be assured," she stopped and continued more slowly, "I have nothing to do with Dan. I don't know who he is, and I definitely didn't know he tried to destroy your life."

"I know. I thought that after he caused the fire, he would never return. I should have listened to you when you told me the truth."

"I couldn't tell you what you wanted to hear."

"To be truthful, Tess, I can't live without you in this house. Look at it. It's not the same. You need to be here with me and fill it with life again."

"Kyle, I'm not going back to the city." She paused until he looked at her. "My parents went home and I am making this place my own. I don't want to be a reporter or a city girl. I want a life with you, sharing it with the meadows and farm animals."

"I have never stopped loving you," he confessed as he took her into his arms. He kissed her and held her securely, closing his eyes knowing he could never let her go.

She revealed, "I'm not always going to be myself, Kyle. I will have times where I'm forgetful or may not feel good emotionally. Are you ready to take on all that?"

"Tess, yes. How I love saying your name. You are not a burden. I don't know what you were like before your accident and I don't really care. Hidden inside you is a woman with heart. I believe in your former life, you loved strong and with all your heart. That is what I love about you, not your flaws and scars."

"What if you get tired of me?" she queried.

"That will never happen. Look at our home. You belong right here with me. This place can never be a home without you in it."

She felt assured, "I want to give you everything I have. Take me as I am and I will always be by your side."

"That is the perfect place to be."

That was how their love mended after being pulled apart by adversities. Tess would never go back to her former life because her true north was with Kyle. They spent many nights gazing at the thousands of stars and planning their new life together. It all seemed so right and picturesque. The last thing they expected was for the past to return, revenge was coming unexpectedly.

Chapter 19

Revenge is Bitter

Dan had been operating from a New York high-rise apartment owned by a friend in real estate. His informant had been spying on Travis and the town he destroyed.

"Hannah, get Jess on the phone and send it through to my office," Dan demanded.

"I tried to call him yesterday for you. There was no answer."

"Has he attempted to call at any time?"

"No, sir. Should I keep trying?"

"No." he sighed.

Jack Hampton, known for his shrewdness, entered the office to give Dan news he least expected. He was a good detective who went bad after Dan offered him work.

"What have you got for me? Jess isn't returning any calls. He's going to hear from me, that good for nothing."

"He won't be getting a hold of you."

Dan jumped out of his chair angrily, "What do you mean by that?"

"Jess gave himself up. Word is out that he confessed everything. Now he's looking at jail time."

"How do you know about that?"

"It's all over the papers. The press also printed something else."

"What?"

"That reporter who was in the car with you was found alive."

Jack handed him the paper with the article.

"She was in the Julian vicinity this whole time?"

"It mentions she went home. But when I drove by Kyle's place last week I saw a woman with him. It could have been her."

"I should have gotten rid of her before she caused all that trouble."

"What are you going to do?"

"I'll show you what! Hannah, book me a flight to San Diego. I'm going to pay Mr. James a visit."

"When would you like to leave?"

"As soon as I can. Get on it! I want to surprise him."

Dan turned to view the city as his blood ran colder. He realized he had fewer people to rely on and needed to get back some of his dignity. Revenge was the best way to decompress his anger. Now that Jess was out of the picture, Dan knew his identity was compromised and he could be facing prison. Avoiding the law while on the run and hiding from crimes executed by his devious mind had been carefully planned, but treacherous. He had reveled in how clever he could be. He would not admit it, but a wave of fear rushed through him for the first time. He was now going to have to do this alone and that meant he had to have precise timing to attack.

Outside of Julian, Henry was on his way to Kyle's place to see Tess and welcome her back. He recalled fond memories of Nathan and Cheryl over the years. Watching their son become a victim of such a devastating crime, created a special place in his heart for him. Approaching the house took him back in time before the fire. Henry and Nathan's friendship was strong with many good times tucked away. The house looked different and he understood why Kyle would renovate it in that way to move on from his loss. Henry could see Tess's touch in the landscaping. Despite her mental abilities, she added beauty to the garden. He walked up a little melancholy and observed that the door was wide open.

"Hey, Henry. Come in," Kyle invited.

"I'd like to say I'm sorry for not coming sooner. It's still hard to come up here. I really miss your dad."

"I miss him too. Tess is here."

"I heard from Marion she came back. I wanted to welcome her. Is she here to stay?"

"This is her home. She wants to stay."

"I love what you did with the place."

"Tess helped out. She has worked hard and put a lot herself into this home."

"Have her parents told you more about her past, I mean about her life as a reporter?"

"No. Tess had her surgery and I met her parents, but not much conversation with them. From what I see, she was a good reporter and was well loved by her community."

"We are all happy she's back."

Just then, Tess came downstairs.

"Tess, Henry came by to see you."

"Hello. It's good to see you again. It's been a while."

"It has. I wanted to say that the whole town welcomes you to the country. We are honored you want to stay."

"I wasn't happy in the city. I finally got Kyle to move in to his house. Although being in the camper was cozy," Tess chuckled.

"I think a lot of us wanted him to move out of that trailer," Henry smiled.

"I'm going to finish making the beds and dusting the rooms. Will you excuse me, Henry?"

"Sure. It was good to see you again." The two men sat at the kitchen table to talk.

"Is she still staying at Marion's?"

"Yes. Occasionally, she comes here to sit and watch the stars with me. She's really changed my world."

"I'm happy for the two of you. How do you like calling her Tess?"

"I still look at her and want to call her Ryan. I had a lot to think about when she left. I want to thank you for showing me what a mistake it was to let her go."

"Hey, this was a good thing for the both of you. I'm sure in her life as a reporter she saw her share of stressful situations. But things are different now. I'm sure she's grateful."

"I'm just happy she came back."

"I got the word back about Jess."

"What did you hear?"

"He is definitely going to prison. He's been in jail before so he will be spending a few more years in a cell. Funny thing, he seemed glad that he confessed. He mentioned that he was on his way to a better life."

"And Travis? How is he doing?"

"Tom said he's taking his community service pretty well. He's always on time and cooperates. His parents are relieved."

"I hated to see him get caught in that trap. He has a good life ahead of him. I hope all of this will be behind him."

"Kyle, the records we pulled up on Dan and his aliases are fairly extensive. He's a man who knows how to get what he wants and get away with it. With Jess and Travis out of the way, well, I would just be careful."

"Do you think he will come back?"

"I can't answer that. Things are closing in on him and he might get desperate. Desperate people do strange things. For now, take care of Tess. Keep her safe." He paused to find the right words, "Kyle, I'm not your dad, but it may be time for you to have a conversation with her parents. It may help you understand and get to know more about this woman you fell in love with."

"Thanks, Henry. Oh, you are welcomed to come by any day. I know if Dad was here, he'd love your company."

"I'll take you up on that. I better get going. Tell Tess I left."

"Drive safe."

Kyle climbed the stairs and poked his head into the bedroom. Watching her make the bed and put the decorative pillows where she wanted them made him smile.

"You look good in this light. With the sun going down right there, the colors touching your face are breathtaking," Kyle complimented.

"You say the most romantic things about me."

"All true, every word."

He put his hand on her arm and she turned to him. They held each other in the dimming sunlight.

"I overheard you talking about Dan."

"I don't want that to worry you. We all care about you."

"I am worried. I don't want him to come back."

"Don't think about that. Henry is working on trying to keep it from happening. You're safe."

"I feel safest right here in your arms. How did I live my life all these years without you?" Tess questioned.

"You know everything that happened changed me and my world for good. I am not saying I was glad you were in a wreck. But I am glad circumstances brought you to me."

"I'm happy I didn't meet you and then have the accident."

"You are going to make many new memories with me."

"I like that better than anything I've ever heard."

"Me too."

They kissed softly as the sun descended over their view of swaying grasses. Tess lit some candles and poured two glasses of tea to settle on the back porch for the evening. Kyle wrapped her in her favorite blanket. From their settee, it was another night to capture forever. It was Kyle's promise to treasure every clear night with her under their stars. He wanted to build lasting memories in her, memories to protect her from the fear and terror since the day her mind changed. Tess learned so much about Kyle, his parents, and the story behind the land they worked so hard to protect. There was a reason why his family loved their land so much.

With the sound of a light breeze and field crickets, Tess looked at Kyle, "You told me all of this was your grandfather's. What is his story?"

"My grandfather inherited it from his dad. It was a small piece of land at first. He wanted to grow hay for the farmers who needed it for their livestock. My granddad was known for his love of animals. He rescued many abused cows and horses in his day. He built a barn over there for them and bought more land out that direction. Those tall trees were still just saplings." Tess tried to imagine the beauty he was describing. "He was picky about who bought the animals from him too. He sold most of them to people he knew. He couldn't live with himself if he put them into the wrong hands."

"You get that from him, don't you? You have the same love for the animals you treat."

"His influence made me love my job. He took care of the folks in and around town. He lived on this place his whole life until he passed away. He was eighty-nine. He lived a good life. It was gifted to my father when he passed and he had that same passion."

"Where did Dan come into the picture?"

"My dad turned this land into the prettiest place in the county, at least that's what my mom said. It left a mark on him and the legacy of his father. There were just so many fond memories of what they sacrificed to keep it in the family. Then this man came by on occasion offering a lot of money for it. Well, as dad put it, 'a lot of talk but never any cash to back it up.' It was always a scheme. He talked about tearing down the barn and

201

the house and then he would give dad more money when he turned it over for a substantial profit and he could get a better piece of land with money left over. Dad was plain about it and said, no. The next thing I knew, Dan threatened him saying there was always another way to get it. He always got what he wanted in due time."

"It was just a threat at that time?"

"We thought so. I don't think he came back until that night the house burned down. Well, we believed it was him. After that, I promised myself I was going to do everything in my power to keep this land safe."

"Maybe it was my fault he came back."

"No, no. He was here before you came into it."

Tess adjusted her quilt and gazed upward thinking about all that had happened to bring her there. She had to shift her mind to where she felt safe.

"It's so peaceful here. I can see why your grandfather loved it."

"You being here makes it even more beautiful."

Kyle took Tess's hand as a shooting star sailed across the night sky. Kyle delayed driving Tess back to Marion's until they realized how late it was.

"I'm sorry I got you back so late."

"Don't be sorry. I want to make that place my home with you. Yes, I said it. I want you to make me your wife someday."

"Oh, I like the sound of that." Tess got out of the truck still wearing Kyle's flannel shirt to keep her warm.

"I'll watch you until you get inside," Kyle said softly.

"Thank you for tonight. I love you."

"I love you, too."

On the lonely drive home, Kyle thought about what Henry said and thought it was a good idea to talk with her parents. He was sure it wouldn't change his feelings about her. But he could glean quite a bit from her history. He was fascinated how her background created the woman he fell for.

Tess sensed Kyle's curiosity to know more. But all she could reveal were small remembrances without detail. In time, she expected to recall more. What was it like to live in Tess's former world of news and media she was so fond of? What shaped her into the person she became? To Kyle, she lacked nothing. He was amazed at her gentle touch and care for him and the animals. It was like he could see inside her and recognize a beautiful soul giving so much for others. Kyle wanted to see where that came from, the past life of Tess Charlton.

"Are you sure it is okay for me to visit your parents without you?" he inquired.

"Yes. I want to stay here at Marion's. I'll be fine."

"I'll be back tomorrow."

"I'll be waiting for you."

They waved goodbye as he made his way down the drive to start his trip. He rarely came into the city and knew no other way to live but country. His old pickup truck stood out among the BMW's and Tesla's he could never imagine owning. The seats in his truck were worn and ripped, held together with gray duct tape. The floorboards were rusted and dirt mingled with dead leaves and straw under his feet. He had hand-crank windows that had seen many hot summers. On the hard steering wheel, his callused hands rested, toned by hard work. His life as a veterinarian was often from sunup to sundown and sometimes late into the night. Five lanes of traffic, a sharp exit, and a few turns later he found their street.

His visit was like no other he had ever experienced. Instead of judging the woman he loved, he wanted to see what she was like. What did her parents love most about her? What made her so passionate? Kyle wanted to relive her history and experience the light where she existed.

Pulling in front of the Charlton home, his truck sputtered once before it turned off. Stacked closely between two other homes, was a beautiful house bordered with flowers and shrubs leading to the entrance. The small lawn was lush and well-kept like the rest of the garden. The one tree was loved and welcomed by guests in flight, birds of many varieties, making their presence known by singing a score only they wrote. Their songs were never the same as they flitted in and out of branches. The windows invited him forward. Kyle was a bit nervous but focusing on the beauty of the home calmed him. Was it where Tess received her love of beautiful things?

Dean opened the door after hearing the strong knock.

"Kyle, so glad you made it. How was the drive?"

"It was different. I don't come down here very often. I am happy to get here in one piece."

"Sarah's waiting for us in the backyard. Can I bring you a drink?"

"Lemonade, if you got some."

"We do."

He couldn't help but look around before asking, "How long have you lived here?"

"Before Tess was born. We still have her bedroom just like she left it when she moved away."

"After she left, did she live close to you?"

"No. She hated the suburbs. She had a high rise apartment in the city just around the corner from the newspaper she worked at."

They stepped outside and Dean brought the drink to Kyle as the ice cubes bounced in the glass. Multi-colored pavers and climbing vines on the wall lent a European feel to the courtyard. Two tall palm trees shadowed a seating area where Sarah waited with a book by her side.

"You had no other children?"

Sarah answered, "No. We were both career driven people and Tess was all we had time for. We put a lot into that child."

"How so?"

"She was always exploring. She loved finding ways to solve little mysteries that came her way. She'd spend hours reading those Nancy Drew books. I swear she wanted to be a detective just like Nancy."

"How did she get into journalism?"

Dean chimed in, "It started in middle school then high school. She won so many awards for her excellence in the craft. I believe she was born with it in her."

Dean took out some old pictures and achievements and set it on a teak coffee table. His face changed expression, knowing she could never be the way she was. Kyle touched each photo and award. He proudly admired Tess with deeper appreciation.

"I love this about her."

She added, "When she lost her memory, it felt like death. She wasn't the same when she came back home. But she was alive and we had to understand that she was here and still our daughter. It was a hard blow for the both of us."

Kyle agreed, "I wasn't able to put the pieces together when I first met her. It didn't make much sense to me and I had to learn to see who she really was. I apologize for that."

"Son, no need to apologize. We didn't know as well. We knew how much she loved being overseas covering events. She wanted the world to hear her voice for the people. She was over in Afghanistan during those terrible wars. We begged her not to go, but she was determined to make a difference for the children and their families."

"How did she end up working for the newspaper?"

"She interned with them before she graduated. Then they found her podcasts and how good she was. She had a lot of followers," she informed.

Dean continued, "She called us one day from the frontline. She had to go into hiding. She was trapped in a small home with concrete floors and no circulation. The room smelled bad. They were practically stacked on top of each other and she didn't know if they would make it out alive. When she called us the next day, we asked her to give it up for her safety. She assured us she was fine and would get home soon. But the worry was too much for us. She's been all around the world and we had sleepless nights wondering if it was the last time we would see her."

"I could understand that. The night I raced to my parents' home as it was engulfed in flames, I was so scared. I lost everything I loved that night. But I'm glad you have Tess back."

"The day she went to Julian, all she wanted was to get justice for those who lost everything, like you and Robbie. That part of her will never change no matter what she goes through. When she came back home, she had a hard time thinking about making new memories and missing out on the old ones. I think you can help her start over. That was why we agreed it was best for her back at Marion's. Her heart was breaking missing you."

Sarah brought out more scrapbooks with photos of journeys and adventures abroad. Kyle looked at every picture intently gazing over who this woman used to be. His hand touched the face that smiled even in adversity and fear. Some images focused on the devastation and rubble surrounded her. Others captured the determination and warmth of the victims Tess loved. Kyle couldn't help but comment on his feelings while he turned each page. He finally sat back and rubbed his forehead, "She put the life back into me. If it wasn't for her, I would have never finished rebuilding my home. My land, the meadows, the night sky, she is part of all of it."

"I know you wanted to know what she was like. But why are you really here?"

"He lifted his eyes and admitted, "Dean and Sarah, I want to marry your daughter. I want you to know that she will always be loved and cared for by me."

"We believe you. She was her happiest when she talked about you, Marion, and those goats in the barn," Dean chuckled.

Kyle grinned, "She loves it out there. She even slept with them." He began to chuckle. "The doe gave birth and she wanted to comfort her. You should have seen her the next morning with straw stuck in her hair after she spent the night with her."

"Really? Did you hear that, dear? Tess never liked animals. That makes me happy knowing she has a tender side for living things, even if it's a goat."

"It was good to visit with you. Reminds me of my folks. Tess helps me cope with the pain."

"Well, if you want our blessing, you got it. By the way, have you heard anything about the man who was in the car with Tess?"

"No. Dale got more information from Jess, but nothing more. I'm not sure where he will turn up if he does."

"Just keep the Sheriff on speed dial, if you come up with anything else; you and Tess need to stay safe."

"I'm just glad Tess lives with Marion until we know more about where he is. Jess said he's good at hiding."

Kyle could see the concern on their faces. They all believed it was only a matter of time before Kyle would face Dan.

Dan's desperate measures were coming together as he planned his meet. What does a man do when he is alone and has no one to do his dirty work for him? The anger stirring inside was more than he could take. His hatred for Kyle and everything he stood for grew with every thought. Dan was selfish and would take anyone down with him who defied him. In his world, it was only Dan, Kyle, and time was running out for the man who considered himself a master of deception.

Chapter 20

Mistaken Identity

Henry acquired new information to share with Dale. He received a phone call from an officer in Temecula. His friend, Joe Cameron was a thirty year pro at finding hardened criminals. His craft specialized in learning about masterminds and what made them tick. He found an address for an Edward Clemens who used to live in Julian twenty years earlier. A search found his face on a driver license. The birthdates matched and the paper trail showing credit cards and a current address.

"It's amazing that you found this," Dale noted.

"It helps if you have a friend in the business. Check out these stats," he shared his email screen.

"What are we going to do now that you have him cornered?"

"We're going to start with a warrant to search his house."

"I can help with that. Let me give Joe a call and we can get it requested. You got him, Hank."

"We know we got him when we see his face in prison for good."

Joe called Dale and with Henry's help, they managed to locate him. They followed him from his job to a local bar. Henry took some pictures of his face and it was plain that his features were the same as the photo ID they studied.

"What else have you got on this guy?"

"You were right. His name is Edward Clemens. No wife, no known family, some who have seen him in the bar says he keeps to himself."

"What is he doing here?"

"Some of these guys with issues are clever at not getting caught. We don't know a lot about this guy, but we can get the warrant and question him," Joe advised.

As soon as the warrant was issued a raid was planned later that evening. They wanted to be sure he didn't escape and turn up missing.

"Are we ready to do this?" Joe asked.

"We're ready."

A group of police officers surrounded the house and Henry pounded on the door at 11:30 in the evening. The porch light came on and they could hear a man coming to the door.

"Yeah, yeah, hang on."

The door opened.

"What's this? What do you want?" Edward asked.

"Are you Edward Clemens?"

"Yes."

The men barged into the house.

"You can't come in here!"

"We have a warrant. We need to ask you some questions about some fires in Julian."

Men were searching the rooms for suspicious activity.

"I don't know what you're talking about. Get out of my house!"

"We have a legal right to be here. Don't be hostile. We have information that you have been in Julian and have been associated with the arsons in the last year. You have also been going by an alias."

"I have nothing to do with that! I'm not answering anymore questions."

"Who's Dan Masters?"

"I've never heard that name before."

"I think you better come with us."

"You're arresting me?"

"You are being arrested for the kidnapping and possible murder of two people by arson. We will read you your rights."

The men handcuffed Edward. Their search uncovered a few personal documents and a passport. Sitting him down in the interrogation room, they began questioning.

"You are required to answer our questions. We have sources who say they have seen you involved in a few of these crimes and you have been evading law enforcement. There was a stolen car with a woman in it who says you were with her."

"I have no idea what you're talking about."

Travis and Jess were behind the unidirectional glass. Dale asked them if that was Dan. They both answered yes. His voice brought back bad memories. Travis remembered hearing Dan on the phone using the name Edward. When Travis asked him who Edward was, he threatened him to never say that name to anyone and to mind his business. There were so many red flags and Travis was grateful to get out while he could.

"I asked you, who is Dan Masters?"

"Yeah, and I told you I don't know."

"Why are you lying?"

"Look, I do have a record. I got into some bad stuff a few years ago. But I never stolen a car or kidnapped anyone." Edward was irritated with the questions and gruff with his answers.

"We have witnesses who say they saw you in Julian a year ago and you got some people to work for you to wreak havoc affecting a lot of people. You obviously don't want to give us a straight answer."

Edward pounded on the table while still handcuffed.

"I don't know who you think you are, but you got the wrong guy!"

"Well, until we can prove you're right, you will be detained."

Joe was annoyed by this man. Everything showed this was the man they were looking for. Why was Edward denying the truth? As they took him away, Joe was perplexed. It wasn't matching up.

"He's hiding something. There's no explanation why he would not fess up."

"Did they find anything else in his house?" Henry asked.

"An old address about three miles from Nathan's place outside of Julian. I intend to find out what's going on."

"I think we got our man," Henry confirmed.

"I hope so. I feel like there should be more clues and evidence."

"After the arraignment, I'm sure there's going to be a hearing. He could be looking at serious jail time."

Edward would stay in jail until they could schedule a court date. There was not a lot of evidence against him and Joe wondered if he had made a mistake. The next day, he decided to have another personal conversation with Edward and get down to business from another angle.

"Why are you here again?" Edward asked.

"I want to know who you really are. Why do all these documents we found say you are Dan Masters?"

"I'm not sure. I had to hire a lawyer to help me get out of jail last time. I never thought I would be back here again. You know I am going to get out."

"You're here for a reason. A lot of people have had their homes destroyed and at least three people died. You could save yourself a lot of grief if you come clean."

"Have you thought that this may be some kind of mistaken identity?"

"You really think I'm going to buy that?"

"Look, I'm a very unhappy person. I have never had a real life and because of that, I struggled to hold down a job and keep a home. I robbed a store and I paid my dues for that. Setting fires is not my forte. I have no reason to be an arsonist."

"Well, I think you do."

"You are entitled to your opinion, but you don't know me. My brother and I spent a lot of time in foster care and it grates on me when you think I'm some kind of heartless person." Edward gave Joe a sarcastic look, not caring what he thought of him.

"Did you say you have a brother?"

"Yeah, he's a twin. I haven't seen him since we were kids. I don't keep up with him in case you are wondering."

"What is his name?"

"Mitchell Clemens. Why do you want to know that?"

"There may be an explanation for all this."

"Whatever this is, has nothing to do with me."

"It has to do with your brother."

"I don't even know the guy anymore. You shifted the blame to Mitchell? Why?"

"I'm not going to point fingers yet. Mitchell may be Dan."

"What an interesting notion. Mitchell taking on aliases? He's a clever criminal. So, does this mean I can go free?"

"Not yet. Unfortunately, we have to keep you here until we get more information. We may need some information from you about Mitchell."

"I don't know anything about him. If I did, I would get my hands on him first for this!"

"I suggest your lawyer help you clear your identity. In the meantime, Dan's still out there. I wish you would have told us you had a brother sooner."

"Why should I? I never cared about that guy."

Edward was sent back to his cell. They decided to get more information about both brothers hoping something new would come up that might clear Edward.

Meanwhile, the man called Dan was making his way to Kyle's. It was getting late and in Dan's mind, there was so much to settle.

Kyle and Tess were coming back from an evening out when his phone rang. It was Dale.

"Hey, Dale. Tess and I are on our way home."

"I just spoke to officer Joe about a man they detained."

"What man?"

"They found Edward Clemens. He confessed to having a brother named Mitchell."

"What does that mean?"

"We are almost sure that Mitchell Clemens is Dan Masters. He is Edward's twin. He may have been masquerading as his brother using his identity."

"Did they let Edward go?"

"No. They still want more information. Dan is dangerous. I hope Joe is getting closer to catching him."

"Thanks for the call."

Kyle was aghast picturing Dan Masters and a look-alike brother.

"What is it?" Tess asked.

"That was Dale. They found Dan's twin brother. I'll explain it later."

"Okay."

Kyle was now more concerned than ever. To think that Dan was using his brother to commit crimes made him sick. His goal was to protect Tess and their home. He needed to focus on keeping her happy despite the worry.

"What would you like to do tonight?" Kyle asked.

"I'm a little tired. Just sitting out on the deck is good for now."

As they turned off the main road onto their gravel road, they noticed a car parked on the shoulder. It was empty.

"Kyle, whose car is that?"

"I don't know. We're in the middle of nowhere. Maybe someone broke down."

Kyle turned on his high beams to see the area clearer and drove slowly toward the house. He was nervous and cautious, making sure he combed everything he could see.

"The lights are off in the house," Tess noticed. As Kyle turned off the engine he cautioned, "Stay behind me."

They walked up to the porch and noticed the door slightly opened. Only the sound of their heartbeat and footsteps could be heard. Pushing the door open slowly, they stepped inside.

"Hello. Who's here?" Kyle shouted.

"I'm scared."

"Hold on to me."

The house felt eerie. Kyle turned on a light and went upstairs to check the rooms.

"Nothing seems to be damaged. Maybe I forgot to lock the door," he admitted.

"What should we do?"

"Get a hold of Dale. Tell him to get here right away. Be quiet when you call."

"Dale, come to Kyle's. We think someone broke in."

"I'm on my way."

As they came back downstairs, Kyle went to the back guest room. Oddly, the door was closed. He heard a faint noise as he turned the handle. Tess was close behind, gripping Kyle's shirt. As he walked in, the lamp light turned on. Stunned, Kyle could feel the anxiety in his chest. Walking in felt risky and there was no guarantee they would be safe. Tess gasped in fear.

"Well, hello, Kyle. The place looks good. So much better than when I burnt it down," Dan said with a cynical smile.

"Why are you here?"

"I just wanted to see you. Oh, I see you have the reporter with you. She sure caused a lot of trouble. She's just as beautiful as the day she almost killed me."

"She did nothing to you."

"She exposed me and my business. Travis and Jess were just pawns in my game and they choked. Tess, you caused that accident and that was a very foolish thing to do."

"Leave her out of this! This is between you and me."

"Funny, that was the last thing your father said to me before he died. Like father, like son."

"Who really are you? I found out you used your brother's name to do despicable things to so many people. You really are sick."

"I know how to get away with it. How do you think I built my empire? You could say, I'm very good at my job."

Dan slowly got up from the chair he was sitting in and approached Kyle. They could see a gun in his hand. Tess watched him come closer. She squeezed Kyle's hand without realizing it.

"Your girlfriend was very close to ruining everything I built. Robbie didn't even see it coming. It's amazing you didn't die in that accident. All I could think about is how much I wanted you dead."

Suddenly, Dan pushed Kyle aside and grabbed Tess by the arm. He jerked her towards him and locked his arm around her neck. The gun metal against her head stopped Kyle from moving forwards.

"Let her go!" Kyle shouted.

"Why would I do that? She's the reason you built this place. She means too much to you now. You obviously moved on from the death of your parents."

"Let her go," he demanded again.

"She's going with me. Now, get out of my way before I take you out."

"Kyle, don't leave me with him, please."

Kyle's eyes darted around for something to stop Dan.

"You got an idea in your head? Don't think about trying to save her."

He backed into the living room with Tess between him and Kyle. She squirmed to get away. Kyle was attentive to how he was holding Tess. He knew a sudden move could trigger his urge to kill her. As he turned his head to avoid a chair, Kyle quickly grabbed the lamp on the table and swung it, knocking the gun out of Dan's hand. Tess stood there and watched helpless. Dan grappled with Kyle until she heard him yell.

"Tess get outside! Run!"

Dan lunged as Kyle kicked the gun towards Tess. On the deck, she tried to call Dale again and did not notice the weapon. Kyle ran to the door. Dan followed and knocked him over and landed a fist. Kyle looked up at Tess outside and knew he had to do this for her. Lying on the floor, he reached as far as he could to grab the weapon. As he stretched, Dan kicked him in the ribs and he fell against the floor. Out of breath, he watched Dan grab Tess by the hair and point the weapon at her, pressing it up against her head.

"This is it, Kyle," he panted, "I'm in control now. This is my revenge!"

"Kyle!" she screamed.

Kyle could see Dan forcefully shaking her. It moved him to push himself to get up. His head and body felt too dazed from the blows to stand. Hopeless, he heard the gunshot. The noise echoed everywhere. Dan was hit and went down. Tess jumped out of the away. She was trembling and looked around.

"What?" Kyle asked in confusion.

Dale moved out of the dark with a rifle.

"Dale!"

"Nothing you could do to stop him from killing. I wanted nothing more than to see him in a cell for life. He caused his own demise. Henry is in the car waiting."

Dale waved Henry in.

"Is he dead?" Henry questioned.

"Yeah. He had a gun to Tess and Kyle took a beating."

Kyle came over to see if Tess was okay. Adrenaline released inside her after she realized Dan was dead. Exhausted, she fell to her knees and Kyle lifted her up, easing her anxiety. She couldn't look at the body lying there.

"No, don't do that. Don't let your power become weakened. He's gone and he will never hurt us again," Kyle encouraged.

She held him tightly as Dale brought her a blanket. He dispatched some of the deputies in the department to come and tape off the perimeter and take Dan's body away. Henry could see it might take some time to recover from the fear and anxiety of the evening.

When it was wrapped up, Dale approached the two. "I'm ready to go now. You think you will be all right?"

She looked up, "I'm hoping we can recover from this very soon. Thank you. I don't know where we would be without your help. He wanted to kill me the day of the accident. I can still see his face. I could have died tonight," she cried.

"You are right, but you didn't die. Please, don't focus on that. We're safe now. Let's not stay here tonight. I'll get your things and we will head over to Marion's." Kyle said quietly.

When they came into the living room at Marion's, she turned and grabbed him around his waist.

"I don't want to sleep alone tonight in my room. Can I sleep down here on the couch?"

"Sure. I'll grab some blankets and camp out on the floor next to you."

Tess seemed to calm down with Kyle close. With him by her side, she was never afraid. Falling asleep, her arm dropped off the edge and her hand touched his. He gently squeezed it and fell asleep.

That next morning, Kyle brought Tess a cup of tea as she rose. Marion had a breakfast sizzling as Kyle told their story about the night Dan died.

"That must have been a frightening thing to go through," Marion said to Tess.

"I'll be fine in a few days."

"I can't stay at the house until they finish wrapping up the report. The whole back deck is a crime scene."

"How long will that be?" Marion asked.

"Maybe a few days, they didn't say."

Just then, they heard Dale's car pull in.

220

"Henry said you would be here. Where can we talk?"

"Yeah. We can go over to the gazebo. Would you like some coffee?"

"No, thank you. Look, Kyle. There is something I want you to know. I didn't want to kill Dan. I did my duty as a Sheriff."

"I know. I really thought I was going to see Tess die before my eyes. It scared me."

"There is second reason why I have been working with Henry on this case."

"What do you mean?"

"Your parents weren't the only ones Dan murdered. I'm pretty sure that man was the guy who killed my father. It happened right after the fires."

"Oh, Dale. I had no idea."

"I didn't know about these different identities he was using. I just knew him as Dan Masters. The whole town knew him that way. My dad was driving by one of the houses that caught on fire. He stopped to lend a hand and Masters was there. Dad called me that night to say he believed it was Dan who started it. They found my father the next day. Ever since then, I worked hard to help Henry find him."

"Looks like justice was served more than once and hopefully we will all recover from the mess."

"It isn't just you and Tess that have to heal from this. I will never see my father again. He was a good man with a big heart. I just wanted you to know my side of it."

"I completely understand."

"Oh, they are releasing Edward today. His lawyer said they won't press charges for unlawful detainment. We let him know about his brother."

"How did he feel about that?"

"He didn't seem to care. They were strangers to each other. He has had a clean record for a while and plans to keep it that way."

"By the way, we recovered a camera in Dan's car. From the looks of its contents, it belonged to Tess. When we are finished documenting it, do you think she will want it back?"

"In a few days, I will ask her."

"Families belong together. Stay strong," he suggested as he turned to leave.

Dale put his hat on, got into his car and gave a little half wave. Kyle took a deep breath and looked out at the horizon, wishing it was all behind them. So many of the folks in and around Julian would be grateful knowing there was little to fear. Closure arrived in time. They have been rescued. Kyle and Tess pitched in to help their neighbors rebuild homes and barns in the following months. Feeling safe, families and friends got together and celebrated. Everyone brought something to eat and someone always brought music to liven things up. The local paper posted an article about the demise of Dan Masters and featured pictures of repaired homes and barns beautifying the land they called home. What seemed like a nightmare became a dream of new beginnings. Townspeople showed their appreciation to the Sheriff and law enforcement at the next town council. Kyle was making plans for a surprise of his own.

Chapter 21

Walking in Fields of Gold

As the seasons progressed Marion's farm birthed new life adding to the number of animals to care for. Some of them were sold to good homes. Marion was always attached to them. She easily pictured Jeb happy to see how far their farm had come. Tess enjoyed it as much. She found that drive from inside and her hard work improved her health. Tess's favorite place was the middle of the field where the wind swept across her face. Her light dress would dance around her and wisps of hair would rise and fall. With her arms outstretched to embrace the breezes, it felt romantic. She could never love the closed-in busy city like that. As she walked back, she pondered over a notion involving Kyle's land. It was about his grandfather who loved different kinds of animals. Tess wanted to pitch her idea to Kyle. She walked inside the shaded barn and sat near the goats she loved so much. They knew her so well and gathered around pressing their noses against her leg. She felt blessed to belong. Most couldn't appreciate the smell and the work it took to care for those living creatures. For Tess, it was calming. It was a place where she learned to adapt to a new memory, a new way of life that gave her pleasure and satisfaction. Marion found her sitting in the hay bed.

"It's amazing how much you love our meadows."

"I do. It helps my mind to feel good. I can't imagine life without it."

"That reminds me of my days growing up on my dad's farm. When me and my sister were kids, we would help Dad pick corn and the cows would see us out there. It was like a signal for them to come eat the removed husks. We could hear them mooing and they would come in groups, even the calves. I used to stand in the fields wishing all the animals joined me. After I graduated from high school, my dad passed away and it was just a ritual to be out in the fields of gold as if he was there. I can still see him. Amazing how much you remind me of myself. I fell in love at a young age. Now I'm old and my time will be done soon enough."

"Marion, don't think that way. I never think of you as old."

"Oh, well, just look at these wrinkles. And I get a little slower each year."

"You know, the animals still gather around you each time you go out there. I'm sure those precious memories come back when you are with them."

"Of course, they do. When I think of you Tess, it saddens me that you no longer have the memories that shaped you. You are still you, but the memories are different. In time, do you think you will want to go back to being a reporter?"

"I would rather be Kyle's assistant at the vet clinic. I have helped him at times. I did get an offer at the paper in Julian to write some articles. It's tricky when I just lock up and I can't write anything interesting. I told them that I appreciated their offer but turned it down."

"You gotta be where you're happy. I have to say, you are your happiest when you are with the goats. Especially this young rascal. Few city folks would sleep in a barn."

"That's true."

"How are you feeling after what happened at Kyle's?"

"Better. We made some changes to avoid reminders of what happened there. I never did thank you for the pillows you stitched for me. They dress up the bed. It's like they have always been there."

"Embroidery was my mama's specialty. It seemed like the right thing to do for you."

"Something still seems to be missing at Kyle's place."

"What could be missing? That house is like a little piece of heaven. Not like my place that looks like it's falling down around its ears!"

"I wondered why Kyle hasn't any animals on his property. It may have been the shock of losing his parents or having such a heavy rebuilding project to focus on. I think it could be the finishing touch for the field."

"You could talk to him about that. It might be what that place needs to make it complete when he's ready."

Tess brought her eyes up to see the sheets blowing on the line. In the other direction the trees waved their leaves softly. She could hear the rustling imagining that they are singing to her. She then looks at the barn. She realized she wanted her place with Kyle to be much like Marion's.

"You know Tess, Kyle's home needs some life. It needs a family, some good cooking, and lots of laughter. Little ones running around making messes. A rocking chair for a new addition to the family. A house full of people is where home is."

"What are you getting at, Marion?" Tess smiled as she looked at her with intrigue.

"Well, I think you should talk to Kyle about that. I love having you here, but you know where you belong."

"I would love all of that, but..."

"But, what? You can't sit around and get it. You have to reach for it. Don't let love pass by. We're not getting any younger. You know I had a full life for years with Jeb and we never had any babies so we took in these critters. You have so much life to live with Kyle."

Marion touched Tess's hand and winked as she stood up and stretched to go back into the house. Codger was lying on the porch and lifted his head for the old woman to pet. It was important for Marion to see Tess have what she deserved. Having lived life, she learned how humans go through troubles and bounce out the other side. She also realized that it made the soul stronger and appreciated deeper. Marion observed Tess growing into a new person. She could never imagine what it was like to be a big time reporter and putting everything into a career like Tess did. The life she discovered gave her room to grow evermore.

She fell in love with the hamlet they called, Julian. The land was quiet yet full of life. She loved how the community gathered for their yearly Apple Picking Jamboree. Among the orchards, gardening, and especially the meadows was where Tess fit in.

Taking her boots off at the back door, Tess had her mind on her future.

"Would you like me to take you up to Kyle's?" Marion suggested.

"He's probably not home."

"I just got off the phone with him and he is waiting for you. Let's go." Marion said with anticipation.

Tess gave the biggest smile getting into Marion's rusty truck. Codger jumped in the back. After the long drive, she stopped and kept the truck running.

"Go on, git going! Your man is waiting for you."

"What about you?"

"Me? You're talking to old Marion. You have a life to start. Now, go girl. Git!" Marion prompted.

Tess kissed her cheek. "Thanks, Marion."

Tess ran as fast as she could towards the front door.

"Kyle, Kyle, where are you?"

"I'm out back."

"What are you doing out here?"

"When I was talking to Marion on the phone, she told me how beautiful you looked standing in the field. I imagined it and wished I was there to see it."

"I have been thinking about what will make me happy. This will be good for the both of us."

"What are you talking about?" He came to her to hold her hands as she spoke.

"I would like us to build a barn and put some animals on the property. We could carry on the legacy your grandfather left behind." Tess suggested excitedly.

"I have thought about that. You know I haven't been in a place to even plan this until you came into my life. But I think you are right. I know the exact place where the barn used to sit. Look, straight ahead over there. Granddad knew the perfect spot to build it. Dad said it was shaded on the southside by tall trees and a breeze found its way to keep it cool in the summer."

"We don't have to build it very big. I want a few goats, chickens, and horses..."

"Hold on. All at once?"

"Well, maybe not all at once. We can start a little at a time."

"Goats first?"

She smiled at him, "That's a good start."

"C'mon! Let's go check out to the spot. Let's make our mark there."

They ran holding hands through the meadow until they reached the location. The sun began to paint the clouds adding hues of orange and pink.

"Right here. This is where we can put the barn. It can come out to here." He grabbed a stick and pushed it into the earth until it held itself up. "And over there, we can put a couple of cows and horses!" Kyle was getting excited just mapping out their project. Tess laughed at him as he gestured and darted around to show where everything would go. He picked her up in his arms as she put her hands around his neck.

"Do you like it? What do you think?"

"I think it's wonderful. I can't wait to start."

He gently put her down and looked into her eyes.

"Tess," he paused and suddenly seemed serious. "None of this would be possible without you. I have been in darkness and swallowed up with grief. You took my breath away when I saw how much those goats loved you. When you were feeding the chickens that day the wind whipped at your dress and your hair moved beautifully. And then, you helped me rebuild my house and turn it into a home. You brought me back from the pain. Now, I want to do something for you; I want to give you everything you want. I want to give you a life with me making new memories. I let life slip by before and I won't ever let that happen again." We belong together and I cannot live without you. Will you..."

"Yes. I will marry you."

Kyle pulled a ring from his shirt pocket. He found it in the safe box that belonged to his mother. Small emeralds surrounding a diamond sparkled as Kyle placed it on her finger. Kyle was in love for the first time. Making Tess his wife was a dream coming true for a lonely veterinarian healing from a crushing fall. With the past behind them, it was time to start a new life together.

Chapter 22

At the End of the Road

Marion heard about the engagement and appropriately shared it with her friends and neighbors. In the same way folks also heard about the new barn going up. Tess planned for a small wedding with just a few close friends and family. Marion was honored that Tess wanted her involved. It was something she always wanted to do if she had a daughter.

Springtime was busy at the vet clinic and Kyle was thinking of hiring another vet to help out. In the past, he insisted on running his practice alone. It was a good time to prepare for his future. He needed time to relax and spend with Tess. He looked forward to being home more and overseeing the care of their own animals.

As the evening was winding down, Kyle received a phone call. He didn't recognize the number and hesitated to answer. After a few rings, he gave in.

"Hello." Kyle said.

"Hey, is this Kyle James?"

"Yes. Who is this?"

"You don't know me. My name is Edward Clemens. Mitchell, the guy who called himself Dan Masters was my brother."

The phone was silent and Kyle didn't know what to say.

"Are you still there?" Edward asked.

"Yeah, yeah, I'm here."

"I know it's a shock to hear from me. I got the news they killed Mitchell. I got your number from Joe. I explained to him why I needed to speak to you."

"So, why are you calling me?"

"Me and my brother were abandoned as kids. We never knew our parents. We were put in foster care then we went to a discipline facility as teenagers. Mitchell was always angry and we both made mistakes. I can see why they thought it was me who killed your parents. But I'm trying to do right and I have been wanting to get my life back. I just wanted to say how sorry I am for your loss. I never imagined he would take it that far, that he would do such a thing."

"I appreciate you telling me that. I hope you keep trying to have a good life."

"Well, I just wanted to tell you that. I truly am sorry. If I could make it up to you, I probably would."

"Thanks."

"Bye." Edward said as Kyle heard the phone hang up.

Setting down his phone, he couldn't believe that conversation. Kyle felt a closure he was longing for all that time. It was brave of Edward to express his condolences and at the same time, chilling to hear a voice like Dan's. After Kyle read the article about the death of Dan Masters, he took a copy of the newspaper with him to the burn barrel. It sat rusted from decades of use behind his shed. He lit it. Looking at the article and picture one last time, he watched the fire consume the photo and words that enveloped his world the last two years. The paper turned to ashes and fell to the bottom. To have the life he wished for with Tess, he had to let all his pain go up in smoke. It finalized the end of a painful story.

"Well, Mom and Dad, it's done."

That was all he said. He walked away knowing it was where he left it, at the end of the road. He turned his gaze to the big tree growing proudly in the front of his house. He remembered Tess looking at this burnt tree. He had assured her it would heal back to its natural beauty. Kyle wanted to do something for Tess before their wedding. He decided to put a swing in that tree for Tess and their children. He took one of the salvaged boards and carved her name on it to use as a seat.

He knew she wanted to have the ceremony outside on their property. Kyle could see her vision and how she wanted to celebrate in her quiet and unassuming way.

He thought about what Dean had said to him earlier. Some of the things about Tess helped him to know the feisty reporter who knew just about everything, writing columns and getting facts down. He could close his eyes and see her in action. He could feel her pain when she tried to protect innocent lives from harm. He could see her nurturing side, a beautiful soul with so much to give. Kyle would always stay close to Tess's parents. Like him, they endured so much without letting it take them down.

Tess survived that crash because she was full of strength and passion. When loved ones have someone who has lost their memory, it feels like they died and they need to get to know someone new all over again. Not so in Kyle's case. He could see Tess was still the person she was before. Some of her lost thoughts would surface at times and he enjoyed seeing what that world was like. He was no longer a young man. He was approaching forty with a new wife to share his home, Kyle wanted a family. Tess was still in her thirties, but to her, it wasn't too late to raise a family in the country.

The day came for the wedding they planned. Watching Tess walk on the cool grass in her bare feet made Kyle smile. No fancy frills or a large crowd. Only those she felt close to. Marion knew she played a part playing matchmaker. She knew Kyle would be happier someday and that day came. After the vows, Digby and Margo smiled for Tess. Her parents were quite happy to know Kyle was caring for their daughter. Lastly, Marion came over to congratulate the couple.

"Call me crazy, but I had a good feeling about you two. From the first time Kyle heard you call him a cowboy," Marion laughed.

"She can call me that anytime she likes."

"I can't thank you enough for all you put up with. I will never stop saying thank you," Tess complimented.

"Oh, no need for that. I believe we all take care of each other. You did my heart good being at the farm. So, I say thank you to you, Tess. You know, I miss calling you Ryan," Marion chuckled and hugged Tess.

"I'll miss you, Marion."

"You'll be visiting, especially after those new babies come along."

Marion said her goodbye with the others and went home. She cried a tear as she drove away, knowing she would go back to an empty home to be alone. Marion did not tell Kyle, but she was sad for a long time after Jeb passed. She got her full smile back when Tess came to her world.

The years have passed and with time, the fields have been filled with animals. Kyle and Tess had two children, a boy and a girl. They named their daughter, Ryan Lauren and their son, Nathan Dean. As Tess hung the laundry, she noticed her daughter running in their field. Ryan would hold her arms out catching the wind. Breezes would blow her hair just like it did for her mother. The children welcomed little ones born in their new barn and at times would sleep in the straw with their parents. Kyle enjoyed being a father. He wanted to teach his children everything about their family land and keep them safe from harm. Tess's mind evaded her old memories. The memories she treasured were more than she asked for. Their past was truly the last memory.

The Last Memory

Annette Stephenson

2022

Also by Annette Stephenson

Divided Mountain

The Landscaper's Wife The Continued Story of Divided Mountain

The Shoe Box

The Tree at Lindley Park

The Many Colors of Poetry

The Other Side of Brook

Made in the USA
Monee, IL
07 April 2023

30993579R00134